THE KINK BROTHERS

THE KINK BROTHERS

LYNN CHANTALE

4 Horsemen
Publications, Inc.

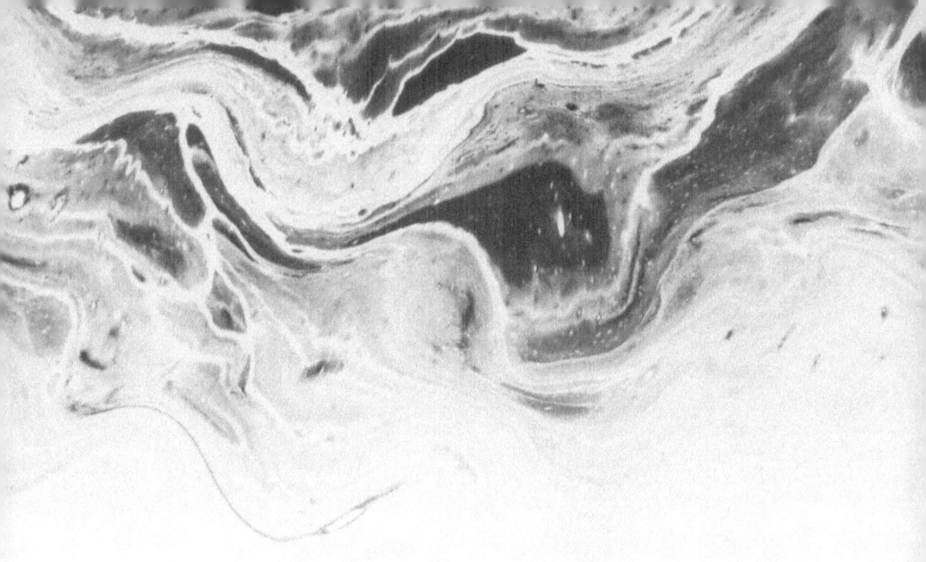

DEDICATION

I'd like to thank my publisher, 4 Horsemen, for believing in me when I doubted myself. Thank you. I'd also like to thank my son, DIW, for the suggestion of an explosion. It made a great diversion in the end. As always, I thank God for the talent.

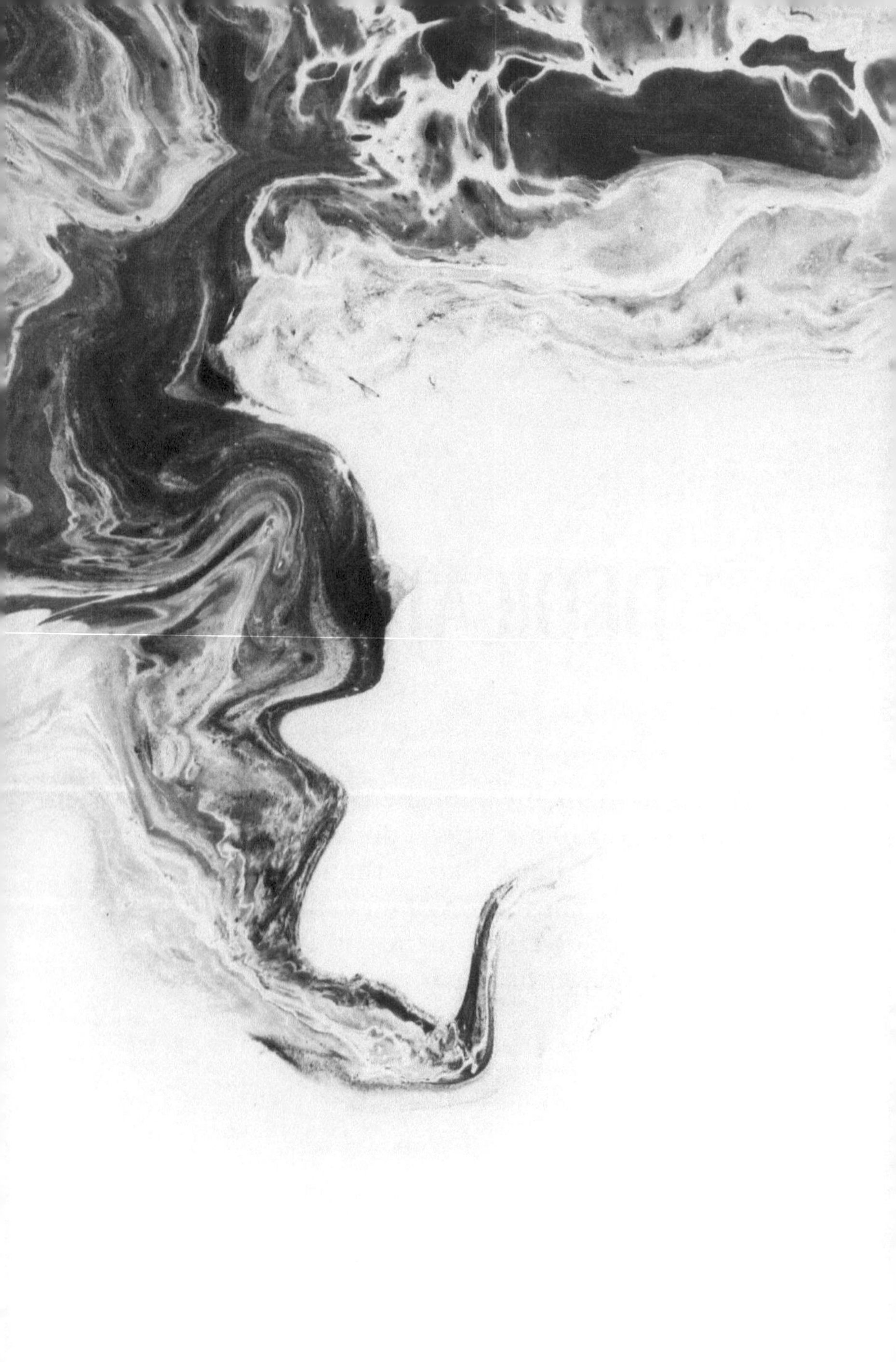

CONTENTS

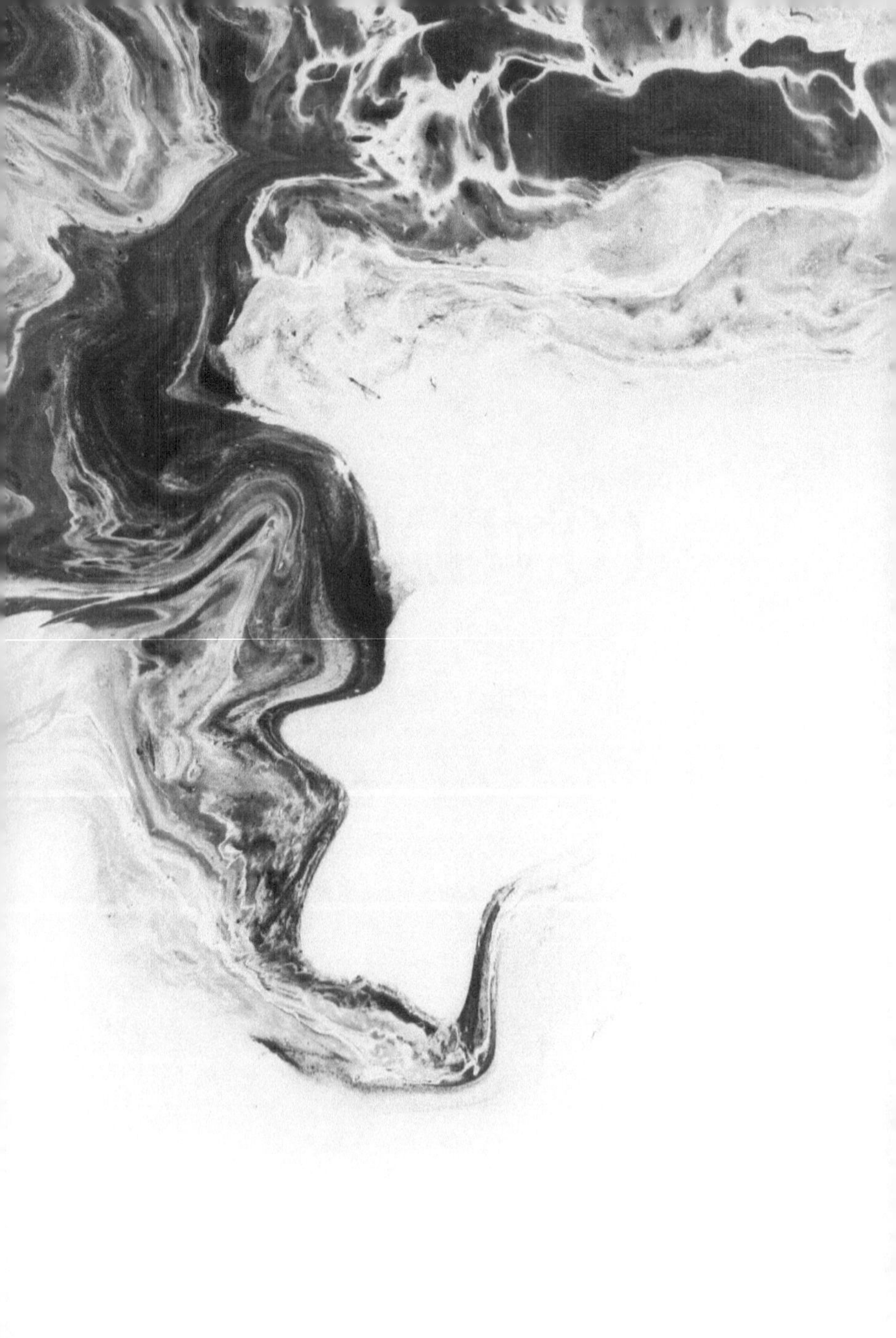

CHAPTER ONE

Waves of heat rose from the red brick street. Israel Asgood winced as he touched the too-hot door handle on the driver side of a sporty BMW. The vehicle, like its occupant, demanded a second and third admiring glance. His car, a newer dark blue sedan, was parked in front of hers. He scanned the sparse sidewalk and car-lined street for any potential hazards before opening the door.

Sweat already rolled down his back and settled in the waistband of his white shorts. He grabbed the bandana from his back pocket, mopped his brow, and returned it to his pocket as he continued to scan the street.

He offered his hand and a smirk to the pretty woman inside. When she smiled back and placed her hand in his, his heart squeezed.

He caught sight of his reflection in her sunglasses. His own sunglasses did little to hide the thin pink line bisecting his right cheek. A long-ago scar from his adventurous youth involving in-line skates, a ramp, and a fence he hadn't wanted to meet. For the umpteenth time he wondered what she saw in him.

She, Cailyn Finch, accountant extraordinaire, intelligent, witty, and beautiful, was the woman he was so in love with he knew there was no one else for him. And he still couldn't figure out what she saw in him.

"You're frowning." Her husky voice poured over him like cool water.

"Am I?" Israel said. "I can't imagine why when I have the most beautiful woman at my side."

And she was beautiful. Flawless mocha skin, dark brown eyes, and full, kissable lips. Even though the day was hot, she looked cool and comfortable.

She smiled, smoothing a hand down the simple floral A-line skirt. The short-sleeve bolero type jacket emphasized her small bust line, and he sighed in appreciation.

"You are such a flatterer." She tossed her long curly hair from her face.

Even as he placed a hand at the small of her back, he moved so his body was between hers and any potential danger. He pressed the clicker and his car alarm chirped. Again he glanced up and down the sidewalk. He looked down to find her grinning at him.

"What?"

"You have this way of making me feel protected without being overbearing," she answered.

A flush heated his cheeks. "You mean a lot to me," he admitted.

And she did. She would be the one woman he would pledge his life to and for. She wasn't just beautiful to the eyes, but to his heart as well. He tucked a flyaway curl behind her ear then caressed her cheek with the back of his knuckles. "I don't want to see anything happen to you."

She held his hand to her face. "I trust you to keep me safe." She raised on tiptoe and brushed her lips to his. "As of now, no one knows what I'm doing."

He pressed a kiss to the back of her hand. "Are you sure?"

"Auditing another accountant's work while they're absent is standard procedure. There's just something off about these accounts."

"If they're as bad as you say they are, TJ can help."

Cailyn adjusted the bag at her shoulder. "Do you really think so?"

He nodded, opening the heavy glass door. Cool air enveloped them as they traversed the narrow foyer. Thin brass mailboxes lined one wall, while a dismal reception desk occupied the other. A hint of lemons, mildew, and overheated electronics swirled in the air.

Israel wrinkled his nose, avoiding the sneeze. Every time he entered the building, his allergies went haywire. TJ needed to tear the whole building down and start from scratch. Another sneeze tickled his nose, and this time, a loud "Ah-choo" blasted the air.

"Bless you," Cailyn said.

Nodding, Israel continued forward.

The entryway opened into a well-worn linoleum space. A door for the stairs was to their right and an old-fashioned elevator was before them.

"What a quaint elevator," Cailyn mused.

Israel barely stifled a shudder at the even narrower elevator. The doors were more of a gate and were closed by hand while the car itself stuttered its way to each floor. He'd gotten trapped in the thing a few years ago and was not willing to take the chance.

"It's one flight up, and they have the entire floor to themselves."

"Afraid of tight spaces?" she teased.

"I've got nothing against Otis," he said, referring to the inventor. "Let's just say I'm not fond of this particular elevator." He steered her toward the stairs, and they managed the short flight.

Israel pushed his sunglasses to the top of his head as the light changed.

They exited onto a landing. Israel grasped the knob. Nothing happened. With a sigh, he pushed the small black button beside the door. At the buzz, he turned the knob and ushered Cailyn inside. Now they were in a long corridor. Industrial beige carpeting muffled their footsteps and gave way to cream-colored walls. He stopped before a double door painted with red-and-gold lettering heralding Red Investigations. He tried the knob. The door swung open on silent hinges. He crossed what could laughably be called a waiting room, although the only thing waiting was a plastic Ficus tree in much need of dusting.

Cailyn shifted beside him. "Are you sure we're in the right place?" She wrinkled her nose and sneezed. "Bless me." She dug in her bag for a tissue.

"Bless you indeed." He chuckled. "We're in the right place. Neither TJ nor Red are big on welcoming visitors."

"Then how do they stay in business?"

They paused outside a white door with no windows. He chose his words carefully. "Word of mouth."

A faint voice reached them through the closed door, and he raised his fist to knock. The next words stalled his fist. "He gettin' his dick sucked." The disembodied voice enunciated each word.

Israel stared at the white wooden door then swiped a hand down his face. The woman at his side stifled a giggle. He resisted looking at her, but a blush heated his cheeks at his friend's candor.

"He's rather frank, isn't he?" she said with a grin.

"Look, mutha fucka, I done told you he gettin' his dick sucked. I ain't walkin' in interruptin' my man's action just so you can cuss him out. So either leave a message with me or call back later."

Israel didn't wait to hear more. He raised his fist and rapped on the door.

"Well call back later. I got company. Enter at your own risk."

Swallowing hard, Israel pushed open the door and prepared for the worst. Papers were stacked haphazardly on what he presumed was a desk. The other indication of the furniture's true purpose was the computer monitor shrouded by more papers and folders.

Shaking his head, Israel focused on the man seated behind the mess. Skinny and black as charcoal. His cinnamon-and-butter-colored dreads were held back by the headset on his head, the mouth piece was pushed to one side. He grinned, revealing two capped gold teeth.

"Rael. What brings you slummin'?" He came from behind the desk and grabbed Israel in a hug. "And this bit of caramel delight. Baby girl, you're the finest thing I've seen on his arm in a long while."

"TJ, this is Cailyn. She needs a little of your expertise on a very sensitive matter," Israel began.

"How sensitive? 'Boyfriend may come out and kick my ass' sensitive, or 'I need to hire a lawyer to keep from being ass raped' sensitive?" TJ asked.

"TJ," Israel admonished.

"What?" The other man's eyebrows climbed his forehead in an attempt at innocence. "It's a legitimate question."

Israel shook his head. He should've known better than to bring Cailyn here, but TJ was the only person he trusted to help in this matter, and if Israel had to endure the colorful speech, then so be it.

"Hopefully neither. I'd research these companies myself, but every keystroke is monitored at work and I don't want to do this from home." Cailyn dug in her pocket and extracted a folded page. "I've worked for this company for a very long time and have never heard of any of the companies listed on that paper." She handed it to TJ. "Anything you can find on them would be helpful."

TJ grinned. "Anything for a beautiful lady." He plucked the paper from her fingers and unfolded it. "So what are you doing with a guy like Israel? I know you can do better than a lowly PI."

Israel held his breath a moment. He and Cailyn had been dating several months, and he'd asked that very question on a near daily basis. He wasn't ugly by anyone's standard, but he wasn't that drop-dead hero gorgeous that women went gaga over either. While he was fit, he relied more on his brains than his brawn.

Cailyn chuckled and glanced at Israel. "He has a certain charm that appeals to me."

He breathed an inward sigh, enjoying the smoldering look in Cailyn's eyes. It spoke to him, and an answering spurt of lust rushed through him. Yeah, this woman meant a lot to him, and that single glance made up for the momentary doubt of not being attractive enough.

"He's always had something going for him." TJ looked at the page. "Where did you say you worked?"

"I didn't," Cailyn answered.

TJ looked up with a toothy smile. "Can't blame me for trying. I recognize one of these names, and I can tell you the company ain't legit. It's a front for something else." He set the paper on the keyboard and went thumbing through the stacks of files on the desk. Several threatened to fall, but TJ seemed oblivious to the hazard and kept searching.

"How do you know?" Israel wondered.

"Red came across this company in one of his exploits, but since it wasn't relevant to his case at the time, he had me file it away."

"You should really invest in a filing cabinet," Israel suggested.

"Then where would I keep my snacks and weed?" He waved to the bank of cabinets obscured by yet more paper.

Cailyn laughed. At the glare Israel shot her way, she covered it with a cough.

"Really, TJ? Man, you need to grow up."

"Just keepin' it one hundred, my friend." He pulled a green folder free from a stack above the computer monitor. "Here we go." He thumbed through the file. "Just preliminary stuff. I didn't trace back who the company belongs to, but it's a front for Lasko Entertainment, which is also bogus." He placed the file on the keyboard as well. "Give me a few days to look into this and the companies you asked about, Cailyn, and I'll get back to you."

She nodded. "Sure. Thank you so much."

"Any friend of Rael's is a friend of mine."

Israel snaked an arm around Cailyn's waist and tugged her close. "Don't get any ideas."

He laughed. "Of course not. I knew she was spoken for when y'all walked in. A woman this fine doesn't stick around just cause you're charming, Rael. There's real feelings involved. Am I right?"

Heat crept up his neck. His friend was just too damned perceptive. "Keep your deducing to the case and not my personal life."

TJ laughed. "Why? When you both feel the same way."

Israel propelled Cailyn forward. "Bye, TJ. Tell Red I'll see him next time. When he's not busy."

"The man ain't been in the office since he shacked up with Gloria. Can barely pry him loose to even do work. Who do you think been runnin' this place?"

"What?"

"Dude's so wide open he acts like it's the first time he done ever got pussy or head. Just shameful." TJ shook his head, a mournful expression on his face. "And because you brought this pretty lady for my viewing pleasure, a ten percent discount from my usual fee."

"Thanks. I'll see you in a few days." Israel ushered Cailyn from the office before the man could say anything else.

"How long have you two been friends?" Cailyn asked as soon as they were out the office.

"Childhood."

"I like him."

Israel swung around, trapping her between his body and the cinderblock wall. A flare of desire ignited in her irises as he pressed closer. "You do?"

She skimmed her hands up his torso then locked her fingers behind his head. "What's not to like about him? He's funny, a tad unorthodox in his business, but he seems to know his stuff."

"You got all that from those few minutes?"

She nodded. "He has a system for filing even if it doesn't make sense to you and me. And he reads people. Very well. So was he right that you have deep feelings for me?"

"Me having feelings for you is irrelevant. You have someone else in your life."

"I never kept that from you, Israel. I've always been honest about the other people I date. Please don't belittle my feelings for you just because I date other people. What I feel for you is real, and I've fallen in love with you."

Her admission squeezed his heart. Here was the one woman he believed he could spend the rest of his life with, but she would never be truly his. So how could he admit how much he loved her and needed her in his life if she couldn't be wholly his?

"And don't belittle your feelings either." She cradled his cheek. "We have more than just amazing chemistry between us, Israel."

He didn't want to admit that she was right, but what else was he supposed to do? "You turn me into knots woman."

She smiled. "Likewise. Whatever I can do to make loving me easier, I'll do, even if it means leaving, but I will not stop being who I am."

And that was another dilemma. He could no more ask her to stop being who she was than he could stop being an investigator. He loved her conviction and confidence. If he asked her to stop being who she was, neither of them would be happy.

"You are an extraordinary woman."

She smiled. "I've been through this a time or two, Israel, and as much as it would pain me to let you go, I would do it to make you happy."

He lowered his head until his mouth was a mere breath from her lips. "You are just amazing, and when you say things like that, I just want to fuck you senseless."

She closed the distance between them and fused her mouth to his. For a moment he was caught off guard, but his body responded to the softness of her lips, the gentle caress of her fingers at the nape of his neck igniting passion as only she could. He pushed her against the wall, taking over the kiss, devouring her mouth as he thrust his tongue inside.

She twined her leg with his. He hiked it higher until his erection fit neatly in the opening he'd created. Her heat tantalized him and he cursed the fact they were in a public place. There was always tonight.

"Let's meet for drinks tonight," he murmured against her lips.

"I'd like that," she said.

Slowly he released her. "Good, then maybe a little something else?"

"I'm looking forward to it." She glanced at her watch. "I've got to get back to work."

He threaded his fingers through her silky black hair. Tonight he would show her everything she needed to know. "We'll talk more tonight."

She nodded and slipped beneath his arm. He followed at a slower pace, watching to make sure she made it safely to her vehicle. Not that he expected any trouble, but ever since Cailyn told him about her discoveries at work, he'd been a little on edge. She didn't see the danger in it, but in his line of work, people had been murdered for far less.

Which was one reason why he'd brought her to TJ and no one else. TJ could find the information she needed and no one would be the wiser. And if by some chance TJ slipped up and let it be known he was looking, the man could take care of himself.

At the short toot of a horn, Israel lifted a hand and waved. Maybe he would do some investigating of his own.

He had his own copy of Cailyn's list. Anything to put her mind at ease.

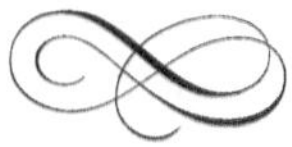

Cailyn Finch ducked her head and hurried back to her office. Low murmurs drifted over the tops of the cubicles. She wasn't late, but she'd been gone longer than she'd intended and she didn't want to do anything that would draw attention to her.

"Can I... Um, Ms. Finch?" a male voice called.

She slowed her steps and glanced over her shoulder. One of the interns—shoot she couldn't remember his name—was hurrying toward her with an open folder and an ink pen. As with times before, he seemed familiar, but she couldn't place why he seemed familiar.

"Yes?"

"I need your signature on these forms? Mrs. Lucas said she couldn't process them without your signature?"

Cailyn paused long enough to examine the documents he proffered. They were the standard travel vouchers for the upcoming conference. She looked them over and scrawled her signature on the dotted line. There was one more step she needed to take.

She walked to the copy machine, laid the documents face down on the glass, and pressed start. Wordlessly she handed the intern the originals then kept the copies for herself. Most of her contemporaries skipped this step or waited for the person who was handing the documents to make the copies for them, but with some of the discrepancies she'd found, she was leaving nothing to chance.

"Ms. Finch?"

"Yes?" She studied him a moment and, for the first time, noticed he was fidgeting with his tie. As well as the imprint of his fingers on the folder. Something about the way he moved. Where had she seen that before?

His gaze darted around before he finally focused on her face. "Is it possible I could talk to you later?" He stepped closer. "I've noticed some things, and well, you're about the only decent supervisor who follows the rules."

She schooled her features in what she hoped was a neutral mask. "Sure. Drop those vouchers off and stop by my office."

He nodded, turned on his heel, and hurried down the corridor.

Cailyn continued to her office. Had he discovered some of the same discrepancies she had, or was there something else he found? *Maybe there was something in the vouchers that caught his attention*, she mused as she unlocked her office and stood just on the threshold.

Stale white walls gave way to industrial beige carpeting. The one good thing she could say about her office was the wall of windows. At least she had sunlight to welcome her and keep the room from being too drab.

She didn't adorn her walls or desk with family photos or pictures of vacations, nor did she have her diplomas on display. She tried very hard to not keep anything personal about her office. Well, her one concession were the potted plants in front of the windows. Two ferns she'd name Flopsie and Mopsie. Both stood sentry in wrought iron stands like bookends.

She crossed to one and removed a yellowed leaf.

Carefully she surveyed her space. Nothing in the office spoke of who and what she was, preferring the anonymity, and now it seemed to work in her favor. Every day she came in and did her job.

Cailyn loved being an accountant. She relished the complexity of balance sheets, projecting a return on investment, or even advising a client on the best way to maximize their bottom line. What she truly enjoyed was finding lost money. That was her specialty. Forensic accounting. Anytime a company needed a special audit, they called her. And she worked very hard to maintain her integrity and ethical standards. Those two things were drilled into her by not just her instructors, but her family as well. If people couldn't trust you with their money, then you couldn't be trusted at all.

So she took all that advice and training and made sure she could be trusted. The only time she'd ever broken the rules was earlier today when she gave TJ the names of the companies she couldn't find.

She crossed the floor, stepped behind the desk, and stopped. Very few items were on her desk, but what was there—the ink blotter, mouse pad, and pencil holder—had been moved. Not a lot, just enough for her to notice that the blotter no longer aligned with the edge of the desk and the ink pen she'd laid across the keyboard before she left was now on the desk next to the keyboard.

A chill walked down her spine. Her office was locked. As were her desk and computer. Had someone accessed any information or found something? She inspected her desk drawers for any signs of tampering. Finding none, she moved on to the computer.

The CPU was farther out than she remembered. She lowered to her knees and examined the back of the unit. Something similar to a thumb drive was sticking out. For a moment she debated on calling someone from IT to come look at it, but maybe this was exactly what she needed.

Standing again, she studied her plants. Now she noticed a bit of dirt beneath one planter. That hadn't been there before she'd left for lunch. She crossed to the plant. Some of the soil had been churned. She smoothed it back into place. Did someone think she was hiding something in Mopsie?

"It's okay," she cooed. She checked Flopsie's dirt. It had sustained the same treatment. "What were they looking for?"

A knock sounded on the door and she turned. The intern, his name stilled escaped her, stood on the threshold, sneaking glances over his shoulder.

"C'min." She brushed the few grains of dirt from her hands.

He quickly crossed the room, pulling a sheaf of papers from beneath his shirt as he approached. "I know enough to know these accounts aren't supposed to be like this." He pressed the pages into her hand. "I was going to bring this to my immediate supervisor, but I overheard him talking to someone on the phone about transferring money into these accounts." He searched her face. "Please. Is there something you can do?"

Cailyn swallowed. "I will give this information to a third party because I don't think my boss would be of any help." She stuffed the pages in her purse. "I'm sorry. I can't remember your name."

He grinned. "It's okay. I'm Paul, and you're the first person to admit you couldn't remember."

"I promise I won't forget this time," she said.

"Thank you." He turned to leave. "Will you let me know if I was right or if I've done something really wrong?"

"Sure thing. Between you and me, I think your instincts are right on."

He nodded and left the office. Cailyn dropped into her chair and blew out a breath. She needed to call Rome, the other man she was dating, and see if he could meet her in the office. He would be able to tell her what she was looking at on her computer.

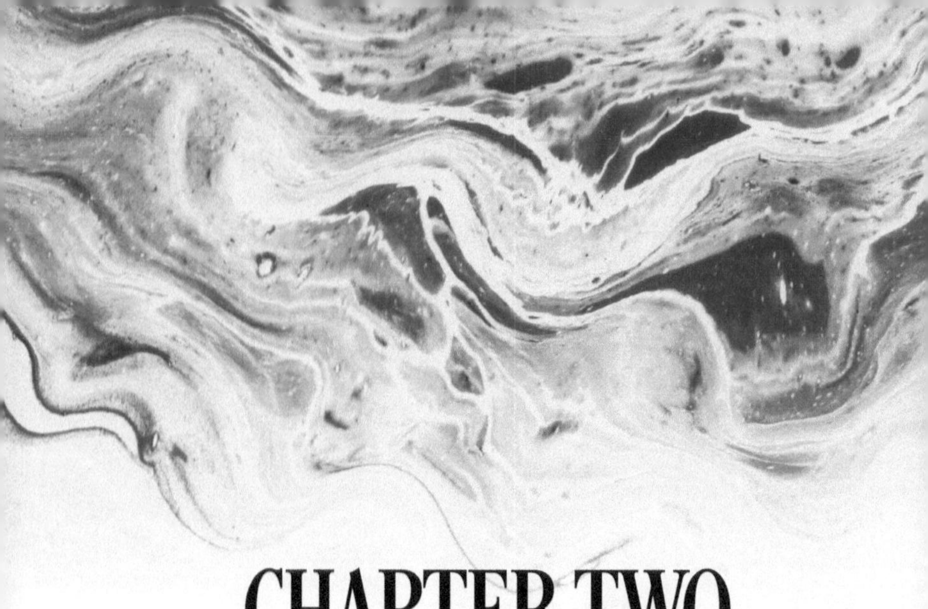

CHAPTER TWO

"**D**id anybody see you?" Cailyn asked anxiously as she ushered Roman Dagon into her office.

"I flashed my badge and had security escort me to your floor," he said, shaking off her hand.

Gasping, she stared at the man. Light brown eyes held intelligence and a flash of humor. Right now those eyes were calm and serious. The strong, square jaw held the faint shadow of a beard. She stifled the sudden urge to trace his jaw, instead focusing on what he'd said. "Are you serious? Please tell me you didn't..."

He chuckled. "No one saw me. And what's with all the clandestine nonsense? You're normally a little more straightforward in what you want."

She poked her head out the door, looked around, and then closed it.

All joking aside, he grasped her hand. Concern stared at her. "What is it? What has you spooked?"

"Well I don't know who may be listening to my conversations at work now, and I'm pretty sure someone tampered with my computer." This was said in a rush.

"Whoa. Wait. Back up." He propelled her to a nearby sofa and forced her to sit. "Now start from the beginning.

She twisted her fingers in her lap, alternating that with plucking at a loose string on her skirt. What did she say? Knowing some stranger had been in her office rattled her. Someone she worked with had rifled through her desk and plants then attached a device to her computer.

Kneeling before her, Rome placed his hands over hers. "Seriously, honey, I'm a little worried. Talk to me." Concern shadowed his light brown eyes.

She held his gaze, not sure how much to tell him about what she'd found or even her misgivings. She licked her lips, noting how he followed the movement. A tiny thrill raced through her, and she was distracted by the answering lust in her veins. What had he asked? Oh, right. The reason she was agitated. "I noticed some discrepancies in a few accounts, and when I brought it up to my boss, he brushed me off. But more than that, someone was in my office. They disturbed Flopsie and Mopsie."

Rome glanced toward the two plants. They looked fine to him. "Are you sure?"

"What do you mean someone copied the files?" an irate voice from outside the office demanded.

Cailyn opened her mouth to say something, and Roman laid a finger against her lips.

"I didn't realize until a few months ago," another more fearful masculine voice said.

"It's bad enough Simpson had to go out of town and I couldn't keep that Finch woman from doing the audit. If I requested anyone else, it would've raised red flags."

At the mention of her name, Cailyn gripped tighter to Rome's hands.

"Does she suspect?"

"I put a tracker on her computer. Whatever she knows, I know."

Cailyn stared at Roman. He motioned for her to stay put as he walked to the office door. With caution, he twisted the knob, pulled it open, and peeked out.

"There's no one in the hall," he said over his shoulder.

She scrambled to his side. "They've got to be in an office nearby," she whispered.

"Do you recognize their voices?"

She listened, hoping for more. She didn't have long to wait.

"So who copied the files?"

"That damn intern copied the files."

"Well find out which one and bring him to me!"

"You can't ham-fist this one. Do you know who that intern is?"

The response was lost when a vacuum cleaner roared to life. They listened a moment longer. The cleaner faded, but no other words could be heard.

Heavy steps signaled the end of the conversation. Rome stepped back and closed the door. "Well?"

"It could be one of the partners." She shook her head. "I can't be certain."

"I don't know what you discovered, but I want to take a look at this device and then get you the hell outta here," he said, walking to her desk.

"You don't think they'd do anything to harm Paul, do you?" She pushed her chair from beneath the desk as Rome dropped to his knees.

"Who the hell is Paul?"

"The intern who copied the files. He gave them to me earlier this afternoon because he wanted me to check it out." Rome disappeared beneath the desk a moment. "I was going to give the information to a third party since no one else in the company seems to think this stuff is serious."

"This is a sweet piece of hardware," he muttered.

"I told the kid to follow his instincts. I could never forgive myself if something happened to him."

"Damn. They can see everything you work on. Capture passwords and get into any files you encrypt. This goes way beyond any tracker or company monitoring I've seen."

"Are you even listening to me?" Cailyn poked her head beneath the desk.

"I could ask you the same question." He crawled out then gained his feet. "If I remove it, whoever placed the device will know, and that will put you in trouble for sure. My suggestion is just to do business as usual, and whatever you need to do, do it on an outside device."

"But..."

"But I wouldn't send an email or an attachment to yourself. It's possible that would establish a link between your PC and the one at work."

"Don't do anything that will draw attention to the fact that there's some hinky stuff going on," she said, straightening. "So what about Paul?"

Rome probed the plants much as Cailyn had done earlier. He picked up the plant, rotating it as he inspected the bottom and sides. He did the same to the second plant. Nothing seemed amiss.

"You have to do something to help him."

"Who the hell is Paul?" He returned his attention to Cailyn.

"Yeah. You asked that already. Intern. Gave me copies. Now may be in danger."

Rome nodded. "Right. I'll look into it, but I don't think they would want to call too much attention to what they're doing."

She laid a hand on his arm and stared into his face. "Please? For me?"

He leaned close and brushed his lips over hers. "Anything for you, baby girl. Get your stuff. I'm not leaving here without you."

Cailyn gathered her purse and messenger bag, stuffing the necessary files inside before she slung the straps over her left shoulder.

"Are you free tonight?"

"I'm meeting my other guy for drinks," she said. She switched off the light, stepped forward, then bumped into Rome's solid chest. "Oh."

They stood there a moment, lost in the electricity crackling and arcing between them. Her door did have a lock, and well, she was attracted to him. By the bulge pressing against her hip, he was very much attracted to her.

"You know, you having someone else has always intrigued me."

"Really?" The heat of his body bled through hers.

"Yes. Do you think your guy would be interested in a threesome?"

Cailyn gaped at him. After her earlier conversation with Israel, she pretty much expected the same from Rome, not him asking for a threesome. "We haven't even had sex yet."

Rome cradled her cheek, brushing her bottom lip with the pad of his thumb. "Stop by my place after your date tonight and we can remedy that."

She pressed her hands to his chest. "I'm not looking for casual sex, Rome."

"Good. Neither am I." He dropped his mouth to hers as if to demonstrate that he wanted more than a fling.

She curled her fingers into his shirt and stepped closer. Sinking into his kiss was like coming home. And with the promise of a night of passion, it had greater meaning. She'd known Rome for a while, but in recent months, they'd decided to date.

From everything she gathered from Rome, he wanted a committed relationship, and not in the traditional sense. Would he find her lifestyle acceptable, and more importantly, would he be able to accept her other beau?

She pulled away. "I need to know something."

He traced her lips with his fingertip. "I can have blood tests and such to you by the end of the week. Until then, I don't mind wearing a condom."

She smiled. "That's... Wow." She kissed him again. "Not what I was going to say, but I can definitely vibe with what you're saying. I really need you to get along with my other guy. I'm in love with him, and I'm not going to just dump him."

"Schedule lunch or dinner and we can all sit down and meet," he said. "If this is what it's like to be with you, then I want to make this a happy moment."

His admission squeezed her heart. Rome made her believe she could have it all. That she could love two men and be accepted and loved in return for her choice.

"I'll do that. Especially if you're serious about a threesome."

Rome held her a moment longer. "Being with you makes me happy, and as long as this guy isn't a total ass, I'll do my best to get along." He paused as he stared at a spot over her shoulder. "I really hope this guy is cool. I tried this with a friend of mine and we haven't spoken since."

Hadn't Israel said something similar? What were the odds both men had the same experience? Then again, with her lifestyle, anything was possible. "What happened?"

He shook his head. "A long, ugly fight that shouldn't have ended a boyhood friendship."

"That bad?"

He nodded. "Let's get you out of here and home for your date." He crossed to the door, eased it open, and poked his head through the opening.

Cailyn waited behind him. When he grabbed her wrist, she followed him out the office, made sure her door was locked, and continued down the hall.

"You don't think you're overreacting?" she asked as they entered the elevator.

He hit the button for the lobby. "Not after that conversation and your obvious concern over this Paul character." He touched her cheek. "They mentioned you by name. Someone was in your office without your permission, and your plants were definitely disturbed."

"Did you find anything in the plants?"

He shook his head.

Was it possible she was overreacting? She didn't think so. After all, Rome heard the same things she had. He'd even inspected her plants. And now he was walking her out the building. He wouldn't go through all this trouble if he didn't think there was some validity to her claim.

She clutched her bag to her chest. In all her years as an accountant, she'd never encountered anything like this.

The most controversial thing she'd found was a business owner hiding funds from the government so he didn't have to pay taxes.

The accounts she'd stumbled upon, coupled with what Paul brought her, was enough to make her look deeper. She had an obligation to her firm, as well as her profession, to make sure neither lost their accreditation or licenses.

"Where are your keys?" he asked as the elevator doors opened.

She held up the fob.

There weren't many cars left in the parking garage. Her BMW sat three spaces from the elevator door, beneath a light and well within range of a panic button. He nodded in approval.

"Do you always park near one of the call boxes?"

"I try," she answered. "I work late a lot. If I can't be near one, then I have a security guard walk me to my car."

Roman slowly walked around the vehicle, even stopping and looking beneath the car every few feet. He dusted off his hands before motioning for her to unlock the doors.

She did so and he looked inside. "You're good." He held her door open.

She stowed her bags on the passenger side then turned back to him. She placed a palm on his chest. "Thank you."

He grinned. "Anything for you." He kissed her. "Don't forget we have a date tonight."

"Wouldn't miss it for the world." She slid into the vehicle and he closed the door. Cailyn brought the car to life with a push of a button then waited for the window to do its thing. "Thank you, Roman."

"Aw shucks, ma'am. It weren't nothin'," he said, adopting a bad southern accent. "It's my pleasure to protect and serve."

She pressed two fingers to her lips then placed those same fingers on his. "See you later."

He stepped away as she backed from the space. As Cailyn waited for the striped exit arm to raise, she spied Roman watching her. A wave of belonging rolled through her. He was taking care of her too. How had she lucked out on two men who dropped everything to make sure she was okay? Smiling, she hit her turn signal and turned right. Maybe over drinks she would share what she'd found with Israel. He had to have more insight than she did. She cast a glance to her rearview mirror, but Rome was long from view. She loved him too. She really hoped a meeting between the two men would be good, because she wanted to keep them both.

Carter Stanley stared out the window into the encroaching night. He'd known since he began his skimming operation that it was only a matter of time before someone caught on to what he was doing. Actually, the only reason he'd gotten away with it this long was due to the death of his predecessor, Barry. He scanned the office. This corner suite had been his and now was Carter's. With Barry's sudden death and the ensuing upheaval, it was the perfect opportunity for Carter to implement his plan. Even with having to find a new co-conspirator, Carter still had many years of extra profit. Now it was all in jeopardy. Even worse was the over-zealous intern and the one accountant at the entire firm he couldn't bribe.

Not that he'd been able to bribe any of the other accountants. In order to secure his current co-conspirator, he'd had to resort to extortion and blackmail.

He turned from the window and glanced around his office. The corner lot. That was his particular hang out. The fact that he had stock options, a bonus, and a very cushy salary wasn't enough to satisfy alimony for two ex-wives and the tuition for the five children all in college. The money he obtained by other means was just for him. Not his money-hungry exes or his sniveling children. The money was all his.

Carter lifted his left arm, pushed back his French cuff, and stared at the beveled face of the Rolex-replica. After the next transfer he'd be able to get his real one outta hoc. As one of the partners in Lockwood, LaMont, Johnson, and Stanley Accounting, he had a certain image to maintain. And appearing broke and destitute was not good for business.

One thing for sure, he needed to know how much Cailyn Finch knew about the irregularities in the accounts. Had she completed the full audit as he suspected? Or were her findings and her report them the only thing she'd done? He feared she would pursue the matter and bring about his ultimate demise from the company and possibly hinder his freedom. Well, he would find out exactly what she knew and see if that intern had mentioned anything to her.

He flexed his fingers. Everything was at stake. At this point he would do anything to keep his freedom, life, and money. He had nothing else to lose.

CHAPTER THREE

Israel ran his middle finger around the rim of the shot glass and tried to concentrate on the news report on the screen at one end of the bar. Cailyn sent him a text saying she would be running late. Concerned something else had happened, he'd called her instead of continuing their back-and-forth via text.

"And you're sure you're fine?" He kept one eye on the television at the far end of the bar.

"Of course. See you soon."

He returned the phone to his pocket and focused his full attention to the broadcast. Normally he watched all the news and read as many physical and online papers as he could handle, but that's not why he was watching now. There was supposed to be something pertaining to his old job.

He raised the glass to his lips and knocked back the amber liquid. A sigh eased past his lips as the alcohol warmed his chest and settled his nerves. Three years seemed like a lifetime ago since he'd walked out on the only profession he could ever truly love, but how could he continue to protect and serve when the very people he worked with no longer trusted him? Even his partner treated him differently after that call and subsequent accident.

At least he had a fallback plan. And he did enjoy being his own boss and not having to follow all the bureaucratic mess that hindered him when he was a cop. He still kept his contacts at the precinct and was pleased to know that his former partner had moved up in the ranks. Other than that, he had nothing to do with his former partner.

They didn't speak anymore. They weren't even friends anymore. Israel signaled the bartender for another drink. Maybe that was a combination of what happened at work and the crazy female they both desired and wanted. No, they hadn't wanted more. *He'd* wanted more. If he could be honest with himself. He could be honest when he wasn't sober. Or if it was late at night.

Or both.

That was the real collapse of their friendship. His insecurity, jealousy. And guilt. He could never forgive the guilt.

Slowly he became aware of a presence at the same time he recognized the faint hint of jasmine.

"Are you starting without me?"

The husky female voice wrapped around him and tightened his groin. And here was a beautiful woman who somehow saw past his flaws to the man he aspired to be. How was he going to deal with not being the only man she loved? Or would this relationship end in disaster too?

"White wine, please," she said as she slid onto the stool next to Israel.

Standing, Israel leaned into Cailyn's soft form. She'd left off the little jacket he'd seen her in earlier, leaving her shoulders bare for his exploration. He skimmed a fingertip over the smooth curve. She shifted, tilting her head and offering him her mouth. He accepted the invitation, sweeping his lips over hers. She melted into him. He always liked that about her. It didn't matter if they were in public or in private, she wasn't afraid to allow her affection for him to shine through. Her fingers trailed up his thigh to stroke his erection. He sighed against her mouth, reluctant to break the kiss.

"Having you here, with me now, makes everything better," he said against her cheek, then he released her. "How was your day at work?" Shifting his erection to a more comfortable position, Israel slid back onto his stool.

"Not too bad."

The bartender returned with Cailyn's wine and set it on a napkin in front of her. She smiled, just a brief flash of teeth, but the man seemed to take that as an invitation.

"This one's on me," he said with a leer. "My shift ends in an hour."

Did this fool not see him sitting here?

"Thanks, but no thanks. I'm with this sexy man right here," she said, resting her hand on Israel's thigh.

Israel couldn't stop the flush of pride and belonging that flowed through him, edging past the momentary flash of jealousy. For extra measure she reached over and twined her fingers with his. He squeezed her hand in return. She was definitely his. What more could he ask for?

"Oh. My bad. I meant no disrespect." The bartender backed away then scurried to help another customer.

Cailyn chuckled.

"What's so funny?" Israel demanded.

"The bartender. He really thought he could start something with me." She shook her head and sipped her wine. "He was hoping to provoke some sort of reaction from you. You were perfect and didn't give him an inch."

She was giving him far too much credit. He opened his mouth to tell her so but stopped when raised voices and breaking glass drew his attention to the far side of the bar. The bartender, who'd just hit on Cailyn, was being dragged across the counter by a large Black man. His beefy hands were wrapped around the ties of the bartender's apron, and the bartender had his fingers on the man's wrists in an attempt to get free.

"Looks like he tried that ploy with someone else." Israel pointed toward the altercation. "Was that the type of reaction he was hoping for?"

"Goodness, I hope not," she said. "I know you wanted to take a swing at him."

"Damn right. I know you're a beautiful, desirable woman, but I would hope other men would have enough respect to not hit on you while I'm sitting right here."

She swallowed another sip of wine. A flicker of something he couldn't define flitted across her features.

"Did I say something wrong? What was that look for?"

"My other guy wants a ménage à trois," she blurted.

Israel sucked in a breath. He hadn't expected her to say that. To buy time, Israel gulped the remainder of his drink. It wasn't as if the thought of a ménage à trois hadn't crossed his mind. A threesome was something he had enjoyed immensely. The energy exuded in one of those encounters was nothing like he'd ever experienced before or since, but that one time had also cost him a friendship and a woman he thought loved him.

"You don't want that?" she asked quietly and placed a hand on his forearm.

He chose his words carefully. "You've been upfront and honest with me about everything. So I can be honest with you about this. I do and would participate, but the last time I had a threesome, I lost two people I cared about."

"What happened?"

"Short version, the woman played me and my friend against one another, and I haven't spoken to him since."

Cailyn was silent a moment.

"Are you sorry you brought it up?"

"I'm sorry that you lost a good friend over a silly female. She took advantage of your vulnerability and exploited it for her own purposes. Did she end up with your friend?"

Israel scratched his head. "Funny thing is, once our friendship ended, she was nowhere to be found."

"Figures." She drained her wine. "Well would you be willing to at least meet my guy? No pressure."

He smiled. "I'd do anything for you, Cailyn. So how did the rest of your day go?"

Drawing in a deep breath, she looked toward the end of the bar. Israel followed her gaze. Two bouncers were pulling the Black man off the bartender while a woman shook her head. Served him right. Men did not like it when other men blatantly flirted with their women. He returned his attention to Cailyn.

"What happened?"

"Not here. Let's go back to your place."

Steam curled around her legs and rose in the shower. Cailyn sighed as the heated spray beat down on her sore muscles. She bowed her head to allow the water to flow over her shoulders. Cool air followed a soft click.

Gentle hands cupped her shoulders then dragged downward. "You are always so tense," Israel said.

"They put a tracking device on my computer at work." She shifted to allow the spray to hit his body as well.

"I figured they would do something like that."

She looked at him over her shoulder. "You could've warned me."

He kissed her shoulder. "Here's a warning. I don't think you should go back to your office without someone being with you."

A moan slipped past her lips as he worked the tension from her back. "That feels so good."

He chuckled. "So I've been told. I'm serious, Cai. I think the information you're pulling can get you into some serious trouble." He turned her to face him. "I don't want anything to happen to you."

She studied the concern shadowing his irises. "I don't want anything to happen to me either."

"Maybe you should stay the night." The corners of his mouth quirked upward.

"We wouldn't spend the night sleeping."

He cupped her breasts. "No, we wouldn't." Israel dipped his head and flicked each nipple with the tip of his tongue. "Maybe a little nightcap before you leave?"

Before she could answer, he was already lifting her. Cailyn placed her hands on his shoulders, wrapped her legs around his waist, and slowly impaled herself on his hard erection. A moan of pleasure left her lips as he stretched and filled her. She loved that moment of oneness.

Cailyn closed her eyes as Israel gripped her butt cheeks. She squeezed her pelvic muscles, and he dropped his head to her shoulder. Slowly she levered up and down, building a slow, sensuous rhythm that heightened his passion as well as intensified her pleasure.

"I love that you're not afraid to please both of us," he murmured against her skin.

"Mmm. I so love hearing you moan." She nipped his collarbone as if to prove her point.

He thrust against her and claimed her mouth. She gave herself over to him, sliding up and down. Each downward stroke made more delicious when he met her stroke for stroke. She controlled the speed of their ride, but he dominated the kiss. Deepening the kiss, his tongue dueled for supremacy. He drank in her taste of fruit and mint. He wanted more. He slid a hand up her spine to tangle in her hair. He jerked her head back to gain better access to her mouth. He wanted to drive into her with the same intensity of his kiss, so he angled her until her shoulders rested against the tile. She shivered against him.

"Oh. That's cold."

He flashed a wicked grin. "I'll warm you up, baby," he promised and pounded into her. Her breasts bounced in time to each of his thrusts. Her nails bit into his shoulders as she strained against him, meeting him with wild abandon.

Israel reveled in the pleasure her body had to offer. She was slick and tight. Hot and oh so tantalizing. Every time he withdrew from her depths, her body fought to keep him. Each time he entered her, it was a welcome return home.

Water pounded against their flesh and steam rose around them. Her cries mingled with the thunder of the shower, or were those his more guttural ones? All that mattered was the ecstasy of the moment, of the joy he was giving her and the pleasure he received in turn.

When her pussy quivered around his dick, he held his breath and stroked just a little harder and deeper. Cailyn tensed in his arms. Rapture and delight crossed her features as she undulated against him. Her startled cry of pleasure was music to his ears and just the catalyst he needed to spark his own ascent into heaven. He gripped her butt cheeks as he slid home once, twice. He shuddered as his climax burst from his body in one pulsing wave after another. He dropped his head to her breast, and she cradled him there, stroking the hair at the nape of his neck.

Slowly he lowered her to the floor, allowing the water to rush over them, their ragged breathing the only other sound in the room. He lifted his head and she met him with a kiss that rocked him to his soul. It seduced and whispered of love and commitment. It promised happily ever afters and mind-numbing sex. It spoke of tenderness and a desire to live the rest of her days with him.

He held her gently, fearing that if he crushed her to him as he wanted, the whispered promise would be lost, washed down the drain with the rest of the water. "You are so incredible. I never want to lose you."

She stared up at him, her dark eyes full of love and contentment, and offered him a saucy smile. "You're not so bad yourself."

He reached past her left shoulder and flicked the handle for the shower. The silence was deafening. Now the only sound was the occasional drip from the showerhead. He pushed open the glass door, grasped her fingers, and led her from the stall.

Once in the bathroom, he grabbed a large fluffy towel from the warming rack, dried the excess water from her body, before wrapping the cotton around her and tucking the end between her cleavage. He grabbed another towel and wound it around her hair.

"Israel?"

He paused in reaching for a towel for himself. "Yeah, baby girl?"

"I love you. Don't ever forget that." With that she turned on her heel and hurried into the adjoining bedroom.

Just like that she managed to sucker punch him again. He didn't deserve her love and devotion, yet somehow he garnered it. He hastily dried off and followed her. By the time he entered the room, she was already in her bra and panties.

Seeing her in this state of dress kindled his desire anew but also left him feeling a tad jealous. Or vulnerable. Either way he didn't like it. She was leaving him to be with someone else. And he wanted her with him.

"Do you really have to go?" Something in his voice must've clued her in on his mood. She set down the skirt she'd just picked up and walked over to him.

"No. I can stay a little longer." She crossed the room to her purse on the dresser. "Just let me send my other guy a text. After what went down in my office, I don't want him to worry about me unnecessarily."

Israel prowled the room, righting the bedsheets and then hanging the skirt and blouse she'd discarded in the closet. Because she spent a few nights a week in his place, she'd started keeping a couple of outfits in his closet. He liked seeing her clothes next to his.

Slowly he rubbed the water from his afro then plopped on the corner of the bed again. He was acutely aware of every click made as she typed her message and the ensuing buzz when there was a response. She'd told him about the device on her computer at work and how she'd asked her other guy to meet her. Her other guy even made sure she got to her car and out of the garage. He'd have to meet this man and thank him for taking care of Cailyn. If nothing else, they did have her best interests at heart.

"He cares that much for you?"

She lifted her head so fast, the towel fell to the floor and her damp tresses tumbled about her shoulders. "Yes. He's offering to make sure I get into work okay tomorrow, but I said that you're taking me."

Israel sat on a corner of the bed. What had he expected, that the guy to be a total ass about her staying? He lifted his gaze and was startled to find her watching him.

"You *are* taking me, right?"

He surged to his feet, the towel falling to the floor. "Of course. I'd never let you walk in that place without some sort of assurance that you made it safely. I'd rather you not go at all, but then that may look way too suspicious."

She smiled. "Same thing he said but without the suspicious part. He just wants to know I'll be safe." *Click click buzz.* Then she dropped her phone back in her purse.

He would never tire of her ability to focus in on him when they were together. This wasn't the first time she'd had a conversation with someone else, but the process was always the same. When she was with him, she was with him. He was the center of her attention, and she made sure whoever was on the other end of the phone knew it. This time whoever was on the other end he had to begrudgingly give props to. The other man cared for Cailyn as much as Israel. Surely that deserved a fair amount of respect.

She approached him, her gaze never wavering. Once she neared, she lifted one arm, extended her hand,

and touched his center mass with just her fingertips. "You need me."

He sucked in a breath. Had he been that transparent? He gripped her wrist when her palm touched his chest.

She applied enough pressure to knock him off-balance. He toppled to the bed behind him, pulling her with him. She sprawled across his chest, cupping his face between her soft palms. "I want an omelet for breakfast."

"You know I can't cook." He grinned.

She nipped his bottom lip. "You're a resourceful man. Figure it out."

He wrapped his arms around her and rolled until she was nestled beneath him. "I am resourceful."

Cailyn welcomed Israel's solid weight. There was something comforting about having him so close. She gently trailed her fingers up and down his spine while he nuzzled her neck. She closed her eyes, savoring the tiny wisps of electricity that rocked her system.

Rome was more than happy to let her stay since she was in a safe place and that was all he required. She hugged Israel, happy that she had two men who adored her and were both almost religious about making sure she was safe. Especially now.

"Are you okay?"

Cailyn dragged her gaze to meet Israel's. He stroked her still damp hair from her forehead. "Yes. I was just thinking how lucky I am to have you."

He flashed a grin. "I was thinking I was lucky to have you." He rolled off her.

She frowned and then shivered at the sudden loss of heat. God, the man was beautiful. Long and lean, his body didn't have a lick of fat on it, but there were plenty of scars. She always wondered where some of the jagged lines and tiny indentations came from, but he never spoke of them. Well, he spoke of one. The scar on his face. The one where he'd nearly lost his eye to a barbed wire fence. Other than that he never spoke of the scars except to say he lived. Still she wondered if they were obtained in the line of duty or somewhere else.

All that sexy skin was unadorned by ink or piercings. He was muscular, but not overly so. She admired his physique as he crossed the room.

"Tomorrow afternoon I'm supposed to stop by TJ's. Did you happen to take a picture of the device? Or better yet, can I bring him by your office to check it out? Computers are his thing and I'm sure he can do some snazzy stuff without tipping off the people who are watching you." He had his back to her as he pulled out the top drawer of the dresser. With one hand on the top of the surface and the other inside, he glanced over his shoulder. "Well?"

"No, I didn't take a picture. But you have to be discreet when you bring him up." She sat up long enough to discard her panties and bra and then crawled beneath the cool cotton sheets. Admiring Israel's form stirred the simmering lust in her veins. Yes, they'd had amazing shower sex, but that was, like, ten minutes ago. "Did you lose something? Or are you trying to find a vibrator to tease me?"

He flashed her a devilish smirk. "That would be in the bedside drawer." After a moment of rummaging through the drawer, Israel closed it with a snap and turned around but stood where he was.

The front of him looked as good as the back. Every muscle in his torso was well defined. The smattering of hair from his belly button down to his semihard dick had her mouth watering. She wanted to lick and nibble every curve and indentation until he begged her to stop. But the rigid way he held his body was not from restrained passion. A bit of wariness wiggled through the desire.

"Is something wrong?"

He offered a tentative smile and shook his head.

Cailyn wasn't sure what he had planned, but that nervous smile made her heart beat a little faster. Did he still have concerns with her other relationship? Or theirs? If her lifestyle had taught her nothing else, it was to be direct and not jump to conclusions. "Then what's on your mind?"

He stepped forward then, clutching something in his fist. "I thought about you." Israel climbed into the bed next to her.

She sighed at the additional warmth and snuggled closer to him. "Okay."

"Close your eyes."

Without hesitation she obeyed. A moment later a small object was placed in the palm of her hand. She opened her eyes and stared at the silver-wrapped package. *This couldn't be a ring, at least not an engagement ring*, she reasoned; he wasn't down on one knee. And Israel was the type of man who would ask on bended knee.

With trembling fingers, she ripped off the metallic paper to reveal a small beige box. Carefully she lifted the lid and bit back a gasp. Nestled in the velvet case were a pair of emerald earrings and a matching teardrop necklace. Wordlessly she caressed the stones. The faint light danced off the facets and gave the room a greenish glow.

"Israel! They're beautiful," she said. "I don't know what to say." She leaned over and kissed him.

He snaked a hand around her waist and drew her on top of him. "I want to see you wearing them."

Cailyn straddled him while she worked the jewelry from its case. His erection hardened beneath her thigh and an answering ache pulsed between her legs. A moment later, with the necklace and earrings in place, she discarded the box.

"I knew they would look stunning on you."

She lifted slightly, grabbed his cock, positioned it at the entrance of her vagina, and slowly slid down. Tonight they would make a memory.

CHAPTER FOUR

Roman twisted the knob and stalked into an office that was more of a firetrap than an office. "TJ. Grab your stuff. You're with me."

"What da fuck? No, 'Hello. Thanks for dinner'? Just, 'Grab your stuff. You're with me?' Mutha fucka, I got my own shit to deal." TJ pushed back from his desk. A few papers fluttered in his wake. "Go. You bother me."

Roman rolled his eyes. "Lunch is on me, but we gotta do this now."

"Man, you know I don't like field trips." TJ folded his arms across his skinny chest and stuck out his bottom lip.

Roman bit the inside of his cheek and shook his head at the childish pout. "I swear you remind me of my three-year-old niece. Tuck your skirt, man, my girl's in trouble."

"This ain't old home week. I can't keep every skirt y'all deem worthy of my time outta trouble," TJ groused. Still he tucked several electronic devices and a manila folder in a messenger bag. "Maybe you need to take up with a good wholesome female who stays outta trouble."

"I think this trouble found her." Roman held the door open for him.

"So where we going?"

"Big accounting firm downtown."

TJ paused in locking the door. A flash of recognition crossed his features. "Downtown."

"You've heard of it."

TJ ducked his head as he pocketed his keys.

"TJ?"

The man shrugged. "I did some research and they came across my radar." He cast Roman a sidelong glance. "Your D-i-D got a name?"

"My what?"

"Damsel in distress."

"Oh. Yeah. Cailyn. She's an accountant at this firm, and someone placed this device on her computer that I need you to take a look at." Roman almost missed the slight jerk of TJ's shoulders. Roman stopped and narrowed his eyes at TJ from across the roof of the car. "You got something you wanna share with the rest of the class?"

TJ shook his head and hastily jumped into the passenger side of the sedan. Roman entered the driver's side at a much slower pace. He pushed the start button, moved the gear selector to D, then nosed the car onto the fairly empty street.

He watched his friend from the corner of his eye. The smaller man held his bag in his lap like a shield. The long, narrow fingers tapped restlessly. TJ was nervous about something and it wasn't this little field trip.

"I said I'd buy you lunch."

"I got expensive tastes," he retorted.

"I think I can spring for more than burgers and fries," Roman quipped.

"It better be Five Guys."

"Hmm."

Traffic snarled and Roman concentrated on avoiding several motorists on their cell phones.

"So have you heard from Israel lately?" TJ asked.

Of all the things to ask.

"Sent him a Christmas card last year. He returned it with a 'Fuck You.'" Roman shrugged. He pulled into a parking lot and grabbed the ticket before the metal arm raised.

"Ouch."

Despite the projected nonchalance, the sentiment cut deep. He and Israel grew up together, went to school together, went to police academy together, and eventually became partners.

No matter how many bad guys they faced or doors they busted down, he always had Israel's back and Israel had his. Until … until that damn woman and the investigation that ended everything...

Roman parked in the nearly full lot he was becoming familiar with and shut off the vehicle. Wordlessly he led TJ into the huge glass foyer of the lobby. They bypassed the empty guard desk and made for a bank of elevators.

"Does she know we're coming?" TJ fidgeted with the messenger bag slung over his shoulder.

Roman cast the man a sideways glance. His old buddy was twitchy in small spaces and with people he didn't know.

"I mentioned I would stop by. Her boyfriend dropped her off this morning, and since it's" he glanced at his watch, "nearly 1, she should be headed to or from lunch."

TJ stared. "She has a boyfriend."

Roman grinned. "Problem?"

TJ vigorously shook his head, the red-and-blond locks dancing. "Your joy brings me joy."

The elevator gave a slight shudder as it slid to a stop and the doors glided open. Roman glanced first one way then the other before exiting the car with TJ in tow. They hurried down the hall to a closed door. Roman rapped lightly on the wood. When there was no answer, he tried the knob.

It was locked.

"I thought you said she knew we were coming," TJ said with a slight whine.

"She does." Roman pulled a small, zippered pouch from his pocket, unzipped the case, and extracted two thin tools. He glanced over his shoulder and set to work. Before TJ could object, Roman turned the knob and pushed the smaller man through the opening. He locked the door behind them.

"Man..." TJ groused.

"Check out the device. Bitch later," Roman ordered.

TJ knew enough to keep his mouth shut. He skirted the desk, pushed back the chair, and pulled out the CPU. "This is one sweet toy, but I have something better." He disappeared beneath the desk.

Roman paced the room. Voices drifted through the door. He tensed. Keys jangled, a soft lilting giggle, and the door opened a crack.

"Thanks so much for the offer, Jill. Raincheck?" Cailyn's voice filtered through the opening.

"Sure. I'll let you catch up on your work," the female voice that Roman presumed was Jill answered.

Cailyn slipped through the door then made to leave it open.

"Close the door."

Roman had to give her credit. The only indication that he'd startled her was the slight bob of her head. She closed the door and then faced him.

"*Roman*, you scared me!" She exhaled noisily. "I thought you were going to text me to let me know you were here."

"I just walked in." He stepped in front of her, lifted a hand, then drew his fingers along the curve of her cheek in a caress. "Are you okay? I know you told me not to worry, but I had to see for myself."

She held his palm to her face. "I'm just fine. My other guy walked me in, and I haven't left the building, since I brought my lunch with me today."

"I'm done." TJ scooted from beneath the desk, stood, and froze.

Roman noted a flicker of something in Cailyn's eyes, and her skin heated beneath his palm. "You two know each other?" he asked.

"I've seen her in passing," TJ said quickly. "You've always had this knack for attracting the most beautiful women." He faced Cailyn. "You have one sweet piece of hardware on your comp, Miss."

"Is there any way to bypass it?"

Roman scrutinized the two. Something was up.

"I worked a little magic, and I'll be able to track whoever tapped your comp when they log on. Just go about your normal workday, but don't send anything personal as pursuant to company policy," TJ said.

She nodded and then turned to Roman. "Paul didn't make it to work today."

"Who?"

Cailyn glared at him.

"Oh right, right. The intern."

"Are you sure...?" Cailyn persisted.

"I'll go by his place again, but there was nothing to indicate anyone had been in his apartment." Roman paused, flicked a glance at TJ. "Do you two know each other?"

TJ knocked his bag from the desk. Several papers scattered from the open bag when he caught the handle.

"Man, this is why I don't like field trips." He waved off Cailyn when she stooped to help. "I start getting clumsy, and when I get clumsy, I make mistakes." He righted the bag and stuffed the papers back inside. "And making mistakes can get me killed."

Cailyn smothered a chuckle and Roman shook his head.

"Check Flopsie and Mopsie," he ordered.

"Da fuck's a Flopsie and Mopsie?" TJ snapped his fingers as he thought. "Wait, that's them rabbits from the kids books. My sis reads them all the time." He glanced around. "I don't see no rabbits up in here."

"My plants," Cailyn explained with a giggle. "The dirt was disturbed."

Heaving an aggrieved sigh, TJ removed a thin wand-like device from his bag and carefully went over each plant. It beeped on the second.

"What was that?"

TJ held up a finger as he studied the screen. He pulled out a tablet, typed, swiped, then placed both back in his bag. "Someone was listening in, but I worked my magic and erased everything."

"Wait," Cailyn began.

"What?" Roman demanded at the same time.

TJ looked from one to the other. "It's done. It wasn't even that sophisticated. I wiped it from here."

"Someone planted listening devices in my plant?" Cailyn swayed.

Roman gripped her elbow. "We're gonna find out who's doing this," he promised. He stared meaningfully at TJ. "Aren't we?"

He held up his hands. "She's your D-i-D. I took care of the computer stuff."

"You took care of it though? You sure you can trace who's watching her?" Roman asked.

TJ sniffed. "Always with the insults. You drag me here and insult my skills." He shouldered the bag. "My work is done. I'll see you downstairs." With that, TJ slipped out the door before Roman could utter a protest.

"He's a strange little fellow," Cailyn said and then wrapped her arms around Roman's waist. She leaned into him. "All of these changes make me think I'm in some strange intrigue. People bugging my office isn't normal. It happens to someone else; not me."

Roman held her close, tightening his embrace when she rubbed her cheek against his chest. "I'm coming by to pick you up after work."

"I appreciate it."

He brushed a kiss against her forehead and placed two fingers beneath her chin, tilting her face toward the light. "You look a little tired."

"I didn't get much sleep last night."

He flashed a knowing smile. "Hmm, how long before I can be the excuse as to why you've gotten little sleep the previous night?"

She lifted on tiptoe and pressed a kiss to his mouth. "Are you ready for that?"

"We'll have dinner tonight and see what happens."

Israel stood in front of TJ's office and scowled at the grungy, grease-streaked "Closed" sign. Israel glanced at his watch. Just after 2 p.m. He knew two things: TJ practically lived in the office, and TJ detested leaving the firetrap for even so much as a sandwich during the day. So where the hell was he?

Israel whipped out his cellphone, ready to call TJ, when footsteps scraping on the cement drew his attention. Israel followed the sound and slid his phone back in his shirt pocket. "Where have you been?"

"Who the hell made you my daddy?" TJ ducked his head, rummaging in the messenger bag draped over his shoulder. "Your lady giving you grief?"

"My lady is just fine. In fact that's why I'm here."

Keys jangled as TJ pulled out a large ring with more keychains than keys.

"How the hell do you find anything in that jumbled mess?" Israel stepped back so TJ could reach the door.

TJ deftly unlocked the door, sliding through the crack as a high-pitched shriek split the air. The sign flipped to "Open" and the door jerked open again.

Israel brushed past him. "I need you to come with me."

TJ heaved an exaggerated sigh. "God, I hate field trips."

"It's for my lady."

A look he couldn't decipher crossed TJ's face.

"What's that look for?" Israel demanded.

TJ opened his mouth to speak then closed it again. "I… Let me just sit a tick."

Israel followed him into the inner office and TJ flopped down in his rolling chair. Israel sat on the only folding visitor chair not covered with a large stack of files. Still, he had to step over a pile of papers just to sit.

"Man, when are you going to get a real filing system?"

TJ glowered. "Don't disrespect my work space."

"I'm just saying. One struck match and this place is gone."

TJ emptied his messenger bag then plugged a device into his computer. Israel watched him for several moments. The other man's fingers flew across the keys as fluently and gracefully as any concert pianist. Israel had to marvel at the almost blurring movement.

"So I need you to take a look at my lady's work computer."

TJ paused. "Can she bring it here?"

Israel shot him a dirty look.

"Man, I'm just sayin'. I just got back to the office, and you know I despise field trips," TJ huffed. He scowled at the continued glare from Israel. "Why are you doing all this extra stuff for her?"

Israel grinned. "She's the one for me, TJ."

TJ looked him over. "But?"

"But what?"

TJ shrugged.

Israel faced his friend. "She and I are good."

"Is that why you're doing this? To make sure she stays around?"

"Please. She doesn't need me to do that."

TJ gathered his messenger bag, pushed by Israel, and then held open the door. When Israel passed through, TJ locked the door. "So you doing this because you genuinely care for her?"

"Yeah."

"The last time you helped a damsel in distress…"

"She was never in distress." Israel spat the words.

They fell silent.

"Heard from Roman lately?" TJ asked quietly.

"Nope." The ice in Israel's voice surprised even him.

"Well. Then by all means, let's see this gadget attached to your lady's computer."

Roman shuffled a few files on his desk until he excavated the one he was looking for. He glanced around the bullpen. Cops in uniform hustled suspects in restraints back to holding. Other cops, in street clothes with badges on their waistband or on a chain around their neck, congregated near a doorway at the opposite end of the hall. That doorway led to the break room and two large urns of coffee. He made a mental note to run to Starbucks and grab a venti nonfat, triple-shot, caramel waffle cone, sans whipped cream.

He opened the folder and sighed. The file contained the notes and findings from the last case he and his partner worked on—the last case he and Israel worked on before Israel left for bigger and better things.

Roman managed a derisive snort. They could've and would've weathered the ensuing investigation from Internal Affairs and even the whispers from their fellow brothers in blue. What they hadn't survived was Nika Cantone.

Just thinking about the curvy, weave-wearing, gum-popping, and oh-so-manipulative female tightened his stomach in knots. He touched the faint outline of a long scar bisecting the knuckles on his left hand. The physical pain had long subsided, but the mental and emotional damage left behind still brought a twinge from time to time. Like now.

He and Israel, as they had done many times before, shared the same woman for sex. The experience was something they trusted one another with, and they only proposed it when he or Israel thought the woman would be receptive. The first time they'd tried a threesome was fresh out of high school and they hadn't looked back.

Nika was different. The first time Roman brought her around Israel, the chemistry arced and snapped between the two. Roman didn't think much of it until maybe the third time they'd gotten together for a threesome. It was then Roman realized Israel had real feelings for Nika, which the woman seemed to return. But there were little things, he conceded. Little things like backhanded insults designed to undermine the friendship he and Israel had shared for more than two decades, and worse, eroded the trust and confidence each held in the other.

Roman sighed and closed the file. No. He'd been aware of what Nika was doing, trying to do, and that's why everything went bad. If he hadn't tried to argue how Nika was playing them both, they would've been more focused on doing their job. Of making sure their suspect hadn't had any hidden weapons. If he hadn't tried to belabor the point, he wouldn't have missed the shiv the perp had tucked away in one of the wide wristbands.

Israel had saved his life. Roman had the scars on the back of his hand and across his collarbone. Screw the partnership. The friendship hadn't survived. Roman mourned that. They'd shared everything as if they'd been brothers.

When Roman learned his mom had an aggressive form of breast cancer that claimed her life five short months later, Israel had been there to carry him through the pain. Pregnancy scares and even paternity tests, they'd survived it all—until Nika.

And now he'd asked a woman for whom he cared deeply for a threesome. Had Israel been around, he'd have asked him. Hopefully the guy Cailyn was dating was half as decent as Israel. The last thing he needed was to try to share a woman with someone he couldn't stand.

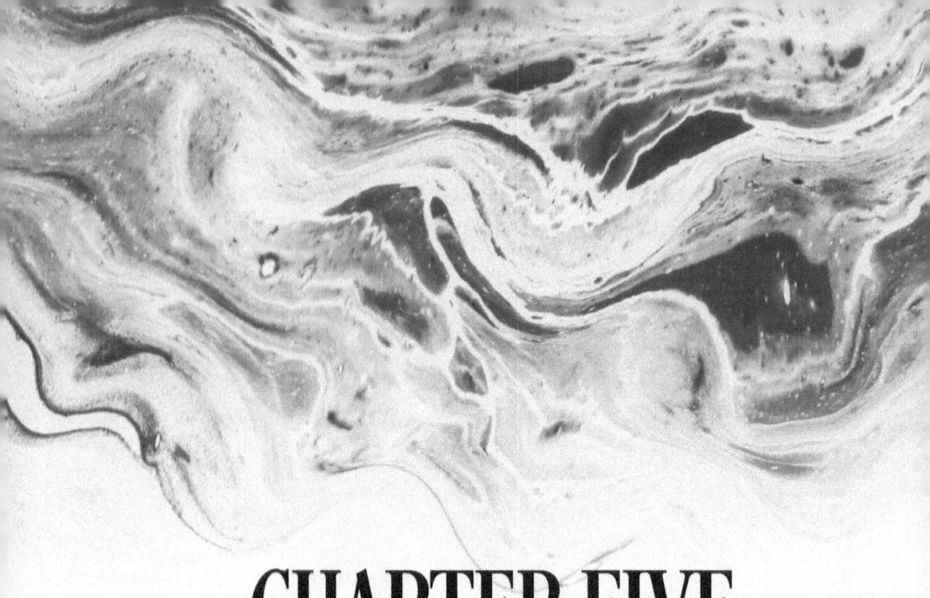

CHAPTER FIVE

Cailyn flashed mild bewilderment and then delight as Israel and TJ crossed the threshold of her office. Israel dropped a kiss on her upturned mouth.

"What a pleasant surprise," Cailyn said, standing. She held her hand out to TJ. "It's TJ, right?"

He grinned. "You're the looker with some serious issues."

Cailyn's smile widened. "I'm hoping you can fix one or two of them." She stepped from behind her desk. "Did you find out anything from those companies I gave you?"

Cailyn wasn't sure what was going on, but some instinct warned her not to bring up the fact that TJ had been in her office earlier with Roman. There was something in Israel's demeanor that intensified that feeling.

"I had to stop by and check on you," Israel said. He touched her face. "You good?"

"Oh, yeah."

TJ dutifully ducked below the desk. "I'm unraveling the financials of one of the companies. It's a really slick setup he's got going on. The outgoing funds aren't large enough to trigger anything. He makes it look like standard payments for product or services. Nearly a quarter-million dollars per quarter is funneled to an offshore account." His voice was muffled as he spoke. "I'm tracking the next payment."

Israel grinned. "I told you he was good."

"I'm the best!" TJ crawled from beneath the desk and then stood.

"I just really want to say how much I appreciate everything you've done." Cailyn held TJ's gaze so there was no mistaking her meaning. "You've gone above and beyond."

TJ flashed a gold-capped smile. "Next time you travel to that Nothing Bundt Cake, hook a brutha up."

She laughed. "Of course."

TJ slipped out the door. Israel placed a hand at her waist. "You sure you're okay?"

Slowly she nodded. "I feel so well cared for between you and my other guy."

"Then I approve that your other male friend is just as concerned about you as I am." He brushed a wisp of hair from her cheek. "He's picking you up tonight?"

"I'm meeting him for dinner," she corrected. "He's working late, and I need to freshen up before we meet."

Israel frowned. "He's not picking you up?"

Cailyn shook her head. "I'm leaving on time for a change." She read the objection in his eyes and she rushed on. "So there will be plenty of people around, and I'm relatively safe."

"Cailyn..."

"Israel. I appreciate everything that you're doing, bringing in TJ and helping, but I still need to live. I refuse to let whoever is at this company intimidate me."

He gave a curt nod. "I just want to make sure you're safe."

"I can call you when I get home," she conceded.

"Any other time, I would be here to pick you up..."

She brushed a kiss over his mouth. "I'm a big girl. I've been taking care of myself for a very long time." She kissed him again. "You don't have anything to worry about."

CHAPTER SIX

Cailyn opened her front door, looked in the living room, and stepped out again, closing the door. *This couldn't be right.* She checked the number on her apartment door. 508. Yep the three brass numbers were still affixed to the wood. She twisted the knob and pushed the door in. The scene had not changed.

Her small sofa and chair were overturned. The rich blue fabric slashed to ribbons, while the fluffy white innards spilled through the cuts like bizarre whipped cream. Glass shards from her cocktail table littered the floor, the light from the hall glaring off the pieces.

Cautiously, she stepped across the threshold. A chill walked down her spine and she resisted a shudder. The space on the corner desk was conspicuously vacant. Her computer was gone. Even the drawers on the furniture hung open, papers sticking out at odd angles. She narrowed her eyes at the blue accordion folder now on the floor. The drawer at the bottom—her locked drawer with her personal documents—was broken and unsalvageable.

She stepped forward, nearly losing her balance on the smooth rolling object beneath her shoe. She righted herself with a hand on the wall. Glancing down, she realized it was the baseball bat she kept in the umbrella stand by the door. The narrow cylindrical object was nowhere to be found, but at least she had a weapon.

As quietly as possible and with the bat on her shoulder, Cailyn moved a little deeper into the apartment. A heavy thud and a soft moan emanated from the back. She froze. Another soft moan made the hairs on the nape of her neck stand up. She glanced around the room then backpedaled toward the front door. Something in the tone chilled her to her core. Violence vibrated, hung in the air. And while she had a pretty good swing, she didn't want to take chances.

She stepped across the threshold, dragging a deep breath into her lungs. Someone had ransacked and robbed her apartment. If that person was still inside, there was no way she was going in alone.

Cailyn walked two doors down then raised the knocker on 506. "Please be home," she muttered under her breath. She shifted the bat at her side and looked at her door. No one had exited as of yet.

"Cailyn! I wasn't expecting you so soon."

She focused on the door at the sound of the smooth mellow voice. The saliva dried in her mouth as a small gasp passed her lips. She'd only been dating Rome the last few weeks, and they hadn't graduated to bumping pelvises yet, which was something she definitely wanted to do. Tonight.

The man was a gorgeous specimen of maleness. All that rich, mocha-latte skin, dewy fresh from his shower. She never realized how intoxicating the scent of man and soap could be until she found herself leaning in to take a healthy whiff. Never mind the overwhelming urge to lick the droplets of water away from the tantalizing expanse of skin. She wanted him to drop the towel.

How many nights had she fantasized about sucking him off? Her gaze traveled the length of his body, past his close-cropped black hair, square jaw, broad shoulders, and perfect pecs, to his muscular thighs and hairy legs, then back to the towel. He didn't seem upset to be caught in such a state of undress, but she really did want that knot to loosen so she could get a glimpse of the delight tenting the cotton.

She licked her lips and firmed her knees in an effort to keep from acting on impulse.

He offered a slight smile, as if he knew how his state of undress affected her. He shifted on the threshold, drawing attention to the fine hairs coating his washboard abs and disappearing into the towel riding low on his narrow hips.

"Cailyn? Are you all right?"

Right now she needed to press her body against his. Would he mind?

"I... Uh..." Why had she come knocking on his door?

"What's with the bat?" Humor as well as concern shadowed his light brown eyes.

Oh that's right. Her apartment. "I think someone is still in my place. I unlocked the door and everything is torn up."

Something unreadable passed through his irises and he beckoned her in. "Give me a sec to put some pants on and I'll check it out."

Cailyn stepped across the threshold and closed the door as he padded down the short hallway to an open door on the left. His place was a mirror image of hers: short foyer that opened into a combination living/dining area that walked into a spacious kitchen. From this distance, she could see takeout boxes on the counter.

She liked the overstuffed black leather sectional and hardwood accents that carried to the ebony dining room table. It screamed bachelor pad, but the colorful woven rugs on the floor and watercolor painting on the ash gray walls softened the purely masculine feel.

"Maybe I should have you wait here," Rome said as he entered the room, shouldering on a holster over the still open royal blue long-sleeved shirt.

She looked him up and down. "I appreciate the sentiment, but you might need backup."

The corners of his mouth lifted. "Right."

She liked that Rome was a cop. Not that she needed him to protect her, but knowing he could protect and serve, like now, was priceless. "I didn't think it wise to go in by myself."

He preceded her from his place to her apartment. "Just stay behind me." Rome paused at her door and looked at her over his shoulder. "I mean it, Cai. Stay behind me."

"Okay."

Rome pushed the door open with his foot then stepped across the threshold, gun drawn. Cailyn stayed two steps behind, the bat gripped with both hands, ready to swing at anyone who decided they were bad enough to dodge a bullet.

She watched as Rome skirted or tried to avoid the majority of the debris on the floor as he crossed the room. Glass crunched beneath his shoe. He paused and shook his head before resuming his search of each room. He disappeared down the hall and into her bedroom.

He returned almost instantly, his face pale, eyes wide, while his lips pressed in a thin, tight line. His weapon was holstered, but his hands were shaking. He dragged a hand over his scalp and avoided making eye contact. He appeared to take several deep breaths before even looking in her direction. Apprehension climbed in the pit of her stomach and she tightened her grip on the bat.

"Rome?"

"You, uh," he glanced over his shoulder toward her room, "better wait at my place. I'm going to call this in."

"But what's in there? What has you so upset?" She moved toward the bedroom, intending to find out for herself.

He grabbed her by the arm as she passed, swung her around, then propelled her toward the living room. "No. You don't go in there."

She jerked away from him. "It's my place."

"Just…" He shook his head. "No. Don't. Just… Just let me handle this and don't go in there."

Something in his irises spoke volumes and assured her whatever had occurred in her bedroom was not a memory she wanted. She lowered the bat. "That bad?"

He nodded.

"All right. I'll wait at your place. I gotta call my other guy and let him know I won't be at home and why."

"Let him know you'll be staying at my place for a few days. I don't think it's safe for you to stay anywhere alone." He led her back to his place.

"That's fine and dandy, but I need clothes. I can't just walk around naked."

A flare of heat filled his irises before he sobered. "I won't complain about seeing you naked."

Cailyn flashed a smile. "Stay focused, Rome. I'm really concerned now. My laptop was stolen, something has you totally spooked, and I don't know if anything else was taken."

He placed his hands on her shoulders and kneaded the tight muscles there. She hadn't realized how much tension she held there until he began the comforting massage. She blew out a breath and allowed the stress to ease from her body. She was safe. For now.

"Look, baby girl. I'm not going to let nothing happen to you on my watch. Me and your other guy are gonna have a nice sit down and talk this through. If he's the man I suspect he is, your safety and well-being is his utmost concern. I wouldn't be surprised if he shows up just to make sure you're fine." He brushed a stray wisp of hair from her face. "Whether you stay with me or him, you will be safe."

"What about Paul?"

Roman's jaw tightened and his lips thinned. "Cailyn, I'm..." He closed his eyes a moment.

A chill shuddered through Cailyn as she thought of the young intern who'd come to her with his suspicions. She gripped Roman's arm. She couldn't bear if something happened to the young man who was just doing his job.

"Is that who's in my bedroom?" she demanded. "Is that what has you spooked? Someone is dead in my apartment?"

Dead was a kind way of putting what had occurred in Cailyn's bedroom. Roman opened his eyes and stared directly into Cailyn's. Fear was uppermost in her beautiful brown eyes, but so was something else. He studied her a moment. Determination.

That sent a wave of respect flowing through him. His woman was no shrinking violet. She would hold her ground if she knew what she was up against. She deserved the truth.

"I don't know who died in there, but it wasn't your friend Paul," he replied. At least he was certain of that. The bloody body sprawled across the foot of Cailyn's bed had been in his mid-forties, not a young twenty-something.

She nodded, some of the apprehension fading from her eyes. "Okay."

"That's it?"

She nodded. "Yeah. I don't think I'd ever forgive myself is something happened to him. He's young and has good instincts. He'll be an exceptional accountant."

"I'll call in a favor and find him for you."

"I appreciate that, Rome."

"And as soon as it's feasible, I'll get you into your place so you can see what's missing. The officers will have some questions for you anyway. They'll want to know what you touched or moved when you walked in."

She nodded. He opened the door to his apartment. "In the meantime, make yourself at home. I'll wait for Homicide at your place."

Again she nodded. Roman waited until she was settled before leaving. Once more Roman wondered what Cailyn had stumbled into.

Israel rushed toward the downtown high-rise and Cailyn's apartment. A hard knot of fear and anger sat in the middle of his chest. It didn't matter that she was unharmed or that she was with her other dude. What mattered was that someone had scared her. Someone had violated her personal space and made her vulnerable.

If he'd been with her, she wouldn't have had to run to her other dude for help. Israel would've been right there with her, making sure she was safe.

He blew out a breath. No matter how hard he fought down the jealousy and insecurity, those ugly emotions always seemed present. Cailyn loved him and he loved her. Why wouldn't that be enough? Why did she have to conform to some ideal? Did her loving another man take away from how she felt about him?

Truth was he was scared. Not of losing her, but that maybe, just maybe, he would never be good enough for her to truly love. But right now, she needed him, and by God, he was going to be there for her.

A couple of white-and-green Sheriff and City of Fort Myers police cars sat in front of the building. As he nosed his SUV into a parking space, an ambulance double-parked and two EMTs jumped out. By the time Israel made it to the lobby, the elevator was full of law enforcement personnel and their equipment. He bypassed them and headed for the stairs.

He burst through the door on the fifth floor just as the elevator dinged its arrival. Israel managed to lead them toward 508. There a uniformed officer stood. He straightened when he spotted Israel.

"I'm sorry, sir..."

"This is my girlfriend's apartment," Israel cut him off. Panic edged in on logic. "Is she here? Is she inside?"

"Name?" came the terse response.

"Finch. Cailyn Finch."

The officer sighed and rolled his eyes. "Your name."

"Asgood."

The officer checked the small notepad from his pocket and stepped aside.

Israel stepped into the apartment and stopped. Personnel bustled about. Some were milling around the living room, but most of the action seemed to be focused toward the back of the apartment.

He studied the scene for a moment, fear gripping his heart. Had Cailyn misspoke? He craned his neck and finally caught a glimpse of his lady. He breathed a sigh of relief. Israel surged forward. She was flanked by two men. One, a bulky man with thick linebacker shoulders and a crop of salt-and-pepper hair on his bulbous head. The other man, tall, lean, and over-tanned, wore a slate gray suit. His partner wore jeans and a sport jacket.

Israel knew both cops and went on point. Someone was dead.

Before he had a chance to ask questions, a man, well-muscled with close-cropped hair and a silk dress shirt open to reveal washboard abs, exited from the back. From the direction of Cailyn's room. When his ex-partner, ex-boyhood friend reached a hand for Cailyn, Israel knew.

Anger surged and boiled over. He charged Roman with a fierce yell. Israel caught him around the middle and the two crashed into an overturned chair, demolishing the remains. Curses and yells surrounded the two men.

"What the fuck is your problem?" Israel demanded before he smashed his fist in Roman's face. "Why do you always go after what's mine?"

Roman managed to get an arm between their bodies and deflected the blow meant for his mouth with a forearm. He deflected as many punches as landed before hands grabbed the two men and yanked them apart.

Cailyn surged forward. "Israel! What—"

"Why is he here?" Israel demanded, jerking against the officers who held him.

Confusion clouded her face. She stepped toward him, hand outstretched.

"She called me for help, Israel," Roman said. He shrugged off a couple of officers as he tried to check his face.

Israel lunged forward, nearly knocking Cailyn down. The officers tightened their hold on him and Roman steadied Cailyn.

"Get your hands off her!" Israel yelled.

"Get him out of here!" the tall detective roared. "We've got enough trouble without this drama, Asgood."

Israel jerked from their grasp and stomped out the apartment. Cailyn looked at Roman and he waved her toward the door. She flashed a grateful smile and hurried after Israel.

"Israel? Israel!" Cailyn called as she hurried after him. He hit the door to the stairs with enough force to jam it against the wall. She winced. She entered the stairwell and he stood at the top of the stairs.

"Is that who you've been seeing?" he demanded.

"Yes, but..."

"Never mind. Are you ok? Are you hurt? Were you hurt?" A least he had enough sanity to ask if she'd been harmed. Even with her standing before him, he wanted to go back and finish pummeling Roman. How could he do this to him? How could she?

Cailyn stood next to him. The anger rolling from his body was palatable.

"Immensely shaken, but we need to talk."

"You're damn right, we need to talk," he snapped.

Eyes widening, Cailyn stepped back. "Why are you so angry?"

"Do you know who that is? What he even did to me?" He spewed his anger over her like boiling acid. Since he couldn't dump it over Roman, Cailyn would suffer. "And he's standing in your apartment like nothing's wrong."

"I know who Roman is to me, but I don't know who he is to you."

"Traitorous bastard." He spat the words.

Cailyn nodded. "So whatever happened involved a woman you two both shared and cared for."

He stared at her, incredulous. Had she not been listening to anything he said? This was Nika all over again. He could've tolerated her seeing any man except Roman. "I can't believe you're with him. I told you what he did, and you still fucked my ex-friend."

She sucked in a gasp, flinching as if she'd been struck.

"You two must've had a good laugh at my expense," he ranted, oblivious to the pain shimmering in her eyes.

For a long moment, neither said a word. Tension stretched as Cailyn clenched and unclenched her fists. Israel stomped in a tight circle, muttering under his breath. A soft sound penetrated and he glanced up to find Cailyn staring at him.

A look of utter sadness ravaged her pretty features. She blinked a few times, the moisture spiking her lashes. When he looked again, anger simmered in her irises.

Shit. What had he done? He held out a hand and she stepped back. "Cailyn?"

She inhaled and the breath seemed to fill her entire body.

"I know you're angry and upset, but it isn't necessary to verbally attack me. We can continue this conversation once you've calmed down."

"I lost everything because of him," he snapped.

"Did you really?" She stepped toward the door. "Chew on this a while. Roman had no idea who I was dating until you attacked him in my apartment." She slipped through the door. The heavy metal slammed, the dull note clanging through the stairwell like a death knell.

Israel swore then stomped down the stairs. *Fuck it!* This day was just getting better and better.

Of all the men in the world, she had to date Roman. Roman was her other man. Roman, his ex-best friend, ex-partner, and ex-everything. At one point they'd been closer than blood brothers. Israel would rush in, and often had, when Roman's more diplomatic style failed to work. And that's what irked him: nothing ever seemed to ruffle Roman's laid-back demeanor. Until Nika. And now Cailyn. He paused in striding across the lobby. No, even when he'd attacked Roman, the man had blocked more punches than anything else.

Roman hadn't thrown one punch.

Not. One. Punch.

That one fact slumped Israel's shoulders as he exited the building and headed for his vehicle. Temper fizzled out until guilt and self-loathing settled in. And he'd taken his anger out on Cailyn. She didn't deserve to be treated that way. His own insecurities were getting the better of him, and now that he knew Roman was involved, it didn't help.

Israel clenched his fists. Cailyn was nothing like Nika, but why did the situations have to be similar? He now knew that what he felt for Nika was shallow and barely lukewarm, but for those few months, she had been his world.

They'd shared so much. The same taste in restaurants, music, vacation spots. When Roman came to him and started in on how Nika was playing them, he refused to listen.

It wasn't until he'd come home to find Nika cleaning out his apartment that he realized Roman was right. By then it was too late. Roman had been injured, almost killed because they'd been arguing over Nika. He'd been put on desk duty until the investigation could clear what had happened, but the worst had been the looks. His fellow brothers in blue had eyed him with more than distrust. No one wanted to partner with him while Roman was on medical. And when Roman returned, the partnership was done. There was nothing left between them except for the goodbye, so Israel resigned.

Even the pleas of a dying woman hadn't helped mend their relationship. That was the one thing he truly regretted. There was no way he could honor Mama Rose's request. There was too much guilt. If he and Roman hadn't been arguing, they'd have noticed the weapon, and Roman wouldn't have been cut up so bad. Israel's guilt was in the way. He couldn't forgive himself for nearly getting his partner killed over, of all things, a woman.

He settled behind the wheel of his SUV and pushed the start button. Now he had to figure out how to apologize to Cailyn for being such an ass. He wasn't sure how he could live with her decision to be with Roman. Could he let her go if it came to that?

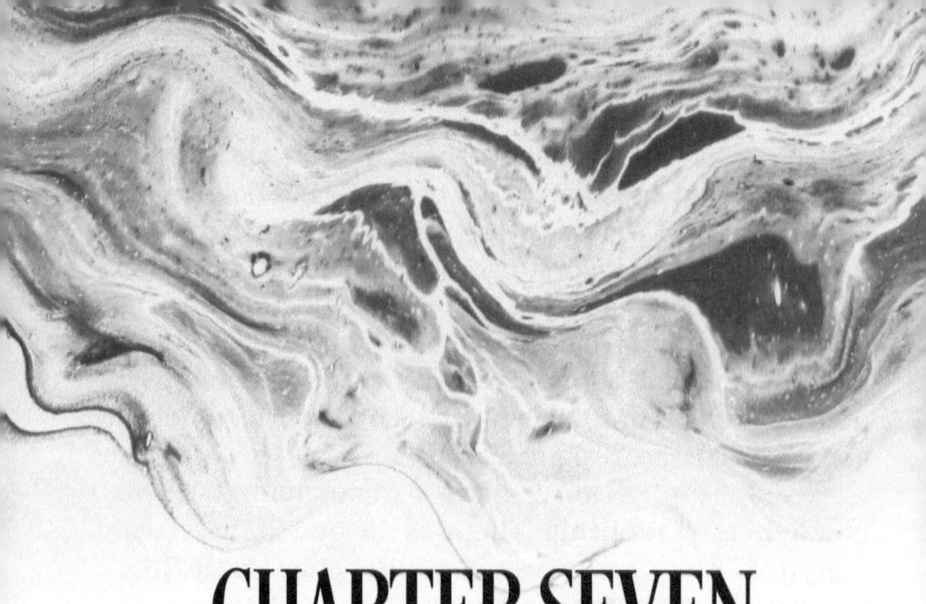

CHAPTER SEVEN

R oman brushed away the concern as he exited Cailyn's apartment. Even the uniform at the door gaped at him. "You sure you don't want me to go after him?"

"Not worth it," Roman said, touching his jaw. *God, Israel hit like a brick.*

At the slam of the door, both men looked up. Cailyn stood in profile. She pressed fingers to her eyes. Her shoulders slumped and an air of despair seemed to hang around her. Temper flared. If Israel had done anything to hurt Cailyn, Roman would find the man and kick his ass. He surged forward.

"Did he hurt you?" Roman demanded as he stalked toward Cailyn.

Startled, she dropped her hands. "What?"

He stopped just in front of her, shielding her from the small group at the end of the hall. "Are you okay?" Concern edged past the subtle note of danger in Roman's voice. As he looked her over, he didn't miss the sheen of tears or the way her lip trembled. Yet he could've sworn there was a bit of anger beneath the tears. Did she cry when she was angry? Had Israel been fool enough to break off the relationship? She didn't seem like a relationship had just ended. He held his breath.

"He's upset and went to blow off steam." Cailyn played what he'd said through her head then frowned. "No. Israel may be a hothead, but he'd never physically hurt me."

Tension eased from his shoulders. Good. Well not that Israel was a hothead, but at least he hadn't dumped her like a fool. Then again Rome would have to take the thought out later as to why he wasn't more upset about the entire situation. He slowed until he stood in front of her. This close, he couldn't help but to touch her. He stroked her cheek. "Why don't we go get a drink and blow off a little steam of our own?"

She lifted a hand to the darkening bruise on his face. "He clocked you pretty good."

"Only because I didn't see it coming." He smirked.

She chuckled. "You didn't hit him back."

"Believe me, I wanted to." Roman draped an arm around her shoulder and propelled her in the direction of his apartment. "Whatever he's told you, I never wanted our friendship to end."

"You both have said the same thing: a woman came between you. Other than that I'm in the dark. Neither of you knew I was dating the other. I didn't know you two knew each other until TJ."

"TJ?"

"You both brought TJ to my office."

Roman shook his head, a short laugh breaking the silence. "Well I'll be damned."

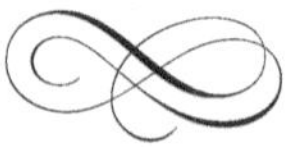

Twenty minutes later they were seated in a secluded booth at El Cozumel, a family owned restaurant, with a bowl of freshly made guacamole and chips. Cailyn gulped a deep swallow of the house margarita, while Roman swigged a Mexican beer.

Of all things, Sunny 106 FM floated from the in-ceiling speakers. He was a little surprised at the more mainstream music but not surprised the restaurant didn't embrace the cliché. The walls were an ecru plaster. No, not plaster cinderblocks. A few sombreros and woven ponchos decorated the space, along with signed photos of city leaders and a few celebrities. Beyond that he didn't care what the place looked like. The food was good and the drinks high-octane. Best of all he was with a woman he'd loved from afar.

"Are you really going to drink all of that?" He pointed to the 40 ounce bowl of margarita she'd ordered.

"I'm gonna give it my best shot."

He scooped some of the guacamole with his chip. "Does that mean I get to carry you out of here?"

"You just want to feel my body."

He sent her a smoldering look. "Any excuse to touch you." He slid his finger along the pulse point in her wrist. "I saw the way you looked at me in my towel."

Very deliberately, she licked the salt from the rim of the glass. His cock jerked like she'd licked him. He swallowed.

"Mmm. You keep doing that and I'll have to arrest you."

"You promise? Handcuffs and everything?" She held his gaze.

He leaned closer. "Are you planning to resist?"

"I could be persuaded."

Desire, thick and palatable, skated between them. He still caressed her wrist, the skin silky smooth beneath his fingertips. Would the rest of her body feel the same? Better question, would she really let him handcuff her?

"You keep looking at me like that and we won't get to eat our dinner," she said.

"You make it hard to decide if I want to eat food or you right now."

She squirmed a little in the seat. "I'll drink a bit more. Then decide what you want to do."

He lifted her hand and kissed her fingertips. "We'll eat. Because I need to explain what the fight was about." He eased back into his chair, reaching for another chip and guacamole.

With that, they sat in companionable silence, munching on the guac and sipping their drinks. Roman waited until their entrees were served before he launched into his version of the story.

"I knew she, Nika, was playing us," he began. "It took a couple of weeks for me to realize what she was doing, but once I did, I tried to tell Israel."

"How did the three of you hook up in the first place?" She brought a forkful of enchilada to her lips. Cheese oozed against the meat and green sauce.

Roman had the grace to blush. "Ever since high school, Rael and I have vibed with threesomes. He or I would find a woman receptive to our kink, and then we would take her home."

"Really?" Delight as well as awe lit her voice. "How fun."

Roman laughed at her reaction. She was the first woman he'd admitted that to who hadn't called him some sort of pig.

Still he touched her hand then studied her face. There was genuine delight, desire, and appreciation. "You really mean that." Now his voice held wonder.

"Absolutely. I enjoy a good threesome," she admitted.

"Well, damn."

She set down her fork. "Did I say something wrong?"

He shook his head. "Every time I think I've got you figured out, you toss something else in the mix." He shook himself. "We'll get back to us, but I need to get this out or I never will." Taking a deep breath, he resumed his story. "Rael stopped by one night while she was at my place and they hit it off. I mean, sparks were flying and they couldn't stop staring at each other." He laughed at the memory, but it was bitter. "She thought she would make me jealous by flirting with him. She was very surprised when I invited her for a threesome."

"Were you jealous when she had feelings for Israel?"

He paused to really consider the question. "At first I was, especially once I realized Israel had fallen hard. Nika never reacted to me the way she did Rael. And yes, I was jealous." He swigged the last of his beer then held up the empty bottle when he caught their server's glance. "So I stepped back just to get some perspective.

"I don't like feeling jealous," he admitted ruefully, "and I wanted to examine why I was feeling this way."

The server delivered the beer, refilled their water glasses, then left.

"We were all at dinner one night. This was after I hadn't spoken to her in a few days. I used seeing my sick mom as an excuse, which she accepted, but I felt like an ass at the time. Anyway, while we were at dinner, I listened to her. I mean, really listened to her talk to us. She'd say things like 'Roman never brings me chocolates like this' or 'Rael shows his sensitive side, why can't you?'"

Cailyn nearly choked on a swallow of margarita at his recitation. Anger on his behalf rose. He touched her hand.

"Yeah, I had that same reaction when I realized what she was doing."

"What a bitch."

He threw back his head and laughed. "Well tell me how you really feel."

"How could she do that?"

Roman wiped his mouth, all amusement fading from his face. "Money. She realized Israel was pretty well off, and she went for the brother with the biggest bank account."

They finished their meal and waited on the bill.

"What happened after you told Israel what she was doing?"

"We argued." Roman dug out his wallet and peeled off several twenties, placing them on the little black tray with the receipt. He stood and offered his hand to Cailyn. She placed her hand in his and got to her feet, albeit a little unsteady, but she held.

"That's all?"

Roman shrugged. "He was in love and he called me jealous because she liked him better." He held the door open for her. They stepped into mild humidity, brassy music, and faint cigarette smoke. "From his point of view, it did look like I was jealous, but I was more upset that she was playing us and that I had brought her to him."

As they navigated the parking lot, he stared off into the distance. "We'd been through a lot. He was there for me when no one else was. If he thought someone was taking advantage of me, he'd knock 'em out. We survived hell week, rush week, the military, the police academy..." He captured her gaze. "We even would've survived Nika, but I got hurt."

Roman opened her door, closing it once she settled in the passenger seat. He settled on the driver's side but didn't start the car.

"How did you get hurt?" she asked quietly.

"We were on a call. Violent ex-con who was notorious for hiding weapons on his person. We were arguing again and didn't take the precautions we were supposed to." He started the car. "The perp had a shiv hidden under his wristband. You know the ones athletes sometimes wear?"

She nodded her understanding.

"Before we could get him in the backseat, he'd cut his restraints and was on me before I could do little more than get a hand up." Roman could still remember the burn as the sharpened weapon swept his knuckles and then his throat.

"A millimeter deeper and I wouldn't be here. The blade nicked an artery. Israel saved my life, but I lost him after that."

Cailyn placed a hand on his thigh. "I'm so sorry."

"The last time I saw him was at my mom's funeral. Other than that, it's been a couple of years since we've been in the same room."

"Until tonight," she said softly.

"Until tonight," he agreed.

They drove in silence. Cailyn turned her attention toward the window, mulling over the events of the day. She stifled a yawn, her brain was a little fuzzy from the alcohol but not enough that she didn't realize they were nowhere near their apartment building.

"Are we going somewhere else?"

"Well, with your apartment in shambles, I thought you might like to grab a few things to make your stay more comfortable." Roman steered the vehicle toward the mall entrance.

She giggled. "You're taking me shopping while I'm a little tipsy? Don't expect me to buy any risqué lingerie."

"My lovely Cailyn, any manner of lingerie privileged enough to caress those sexy curves will be risqué." He squeezed her hand. "You just leave that part of the hunt to me."

She smirked. "Oh really?"

He found a parking space near one of the entrances and maneuvered the car between the white lines. "I know what I like to see my woman in."

"So now I'm yours?"

Roman nodded. "Even with Israel lurking in the wings, you're mine." He stepped out and then hurried to her side to open the door. "And I always take care of what's mine."

Israel sat on the edge of the bed and stared at the open closet. Just the night before, he'd gotten little sleep because Cailyn gave him something no woman ever had before, and tonight he was sleeping alone. Not that she had planned to spend the evening with him, but maybe she would've had he handled things better. How was he supposed to handle things when Roman was her other man?

He flexed his sore knuckles, the skin split and a little bruised. Roman had every right to press charges, and he hadn't. Could Israel have been so gracious had the roles been reversed? Probably not. Then he'd taken a swipe at Cailyn.

He fell back on the bed and draped his arm over his eyes. She hadn't known, and she'd been an easy target. Would she be angry with him? No, not angry. Hurt. He'd hurt her with his callousness, when all she'd tried to do was comfort him, wanted to understand the situation, and he'd accused her of laughing at him. He groaned. He could kick his own ass for being a dick.

Israel bolted upright. Someone was dead in Cailyn's apartment.

He scrambled for his phone and punched in the number to someone he hoped would still talk to him.

"Jenkins."

"J, it's Rael."

Silence greeted him before a cough filled the line. "Fool, what you doing calling me at work?"

"Your work is the reason I'm calling,"

Voices grew louder then quieted. "I heard about your scuffle at the crime scene. You lucky the lieutenant didn't haul you in."

"What can you tell me about the vic?"

"Not my case," Jenkins said.

"C'mon, Jenkins. Has the body been identified?"

Silence.

"Jenkins. It's a simple question."

"Look, it's one thing to give you inside info on a missing person or a tidbit from a cold case, which you've helped us close plenty since you've been a PI, but this is an active investigation and it isn't mine."

Israel huffed. "All right. What can you tell me?"

"He died violently."

Israel disconnected the call. If he couldn't get anything from the cops, then maybe he'd try his contact at the morgue. Molly owed him a favor.

"I can so get fired for this," Molly Gannon said as she opened one of the numbered drawers which held a body.

"I won't say anything if you don't."

She shook her head. "You owe me big time for this."

The lights were low in the autopsy room. Strong antiseptic scented the air, with an undercurrent of death. Israel was not keen on seeing the dead body, but he needed to know who it was if he was going to help Cailyn.

"All right, lemme see." He braced for the worst but was still unprepared for the brutality of death. The medical examiner had not yet gotten to the man, or what he presumed was a man. Dried splattered blood was caked and matted in what had been sandy brown hair. The skull was misshapen, and Israel could see bits of bone and gray matter around a small wound.

Israel closed his eyes and knew he would be seeing this sight in his dreams for a great many nights to come. "Has he been identified?"

Molly glanced at the tag on the drawer. "Spencer Avery. Now you really have to leave. The ME will be in soon to start the autopsy, and the last thing you want is to be here when they do."

Israel nodded. "Keep me in the loop, Molly. If they find something, let me know."

"You better come with a damn good bribe."

He kissed her cheek. "Have I ever let you down?" He turned from the drawer, not wanting her to see just how queasy the sight had made him.

"I want something shiny!" she called after him.

He smiled, heard faint voices in the corridor, and hurried the other way. He ducked into a bathroom and availed himself of an empty stall where he promptly threw up. At least he had a name. He could use his resources to find out more about Spencer Avery. Then he was gonna get drunk.

TJ hunkered behind his desk, idly strumming his fingers on his thigh to the driving metal beat of "Bodies" by Hollywood Undead. Six flatscreen monitors lit the room. One was dedicated to the security cameras he'd placed around his property, and that screen was broken into ten smaller boxes, not a single blind spot existing in the cameras. Two monitors held code in various states, and one was dedicated to a mass multiplayer computer game, Ark. One was dedicated to the darkness, and the other two were streaming the information from Israel and Roman's D-i-D.

He had to stifle a snort that both men were obviously in love with the same woman and yet had no idea they were both helping her with the same case. He glanced at the security monitor and spied a heavy-set man with two ponytails on either side of his round face. He held up a keycard. The light over the door blinked red then green. He pushed into the foyer and waited.

TJ tapped a few keys and the man's moon face filled the screen. Normally once the first door closed, the second door would open, but TJ had a score to settle with his partner for leaving him to run the office for the last few weeks while the man played house.

"Stop fucking around, TJ," Bruno "Red" Carrothers barked.

"That's my line, Red," TJ retorted.

"I ain't in the mood." He banged a meaty fist on the glass door, but it didn't budge.

"She had enough of your lovin'?"

Red slammed his fist against the door. "TJ!"

TJ grinned then typed a few keys to release the lock. He followed Red's progress on the monitors until the man stomped into the office. "'Bout fucking time you decided to show up. Your clients have been antsy." He shoved a folder at Bruno. "It's a good thing I'm damn good at what I do or else your ass and rep would be on the street right now."

Bruno snorted. "Yeah, like I know you've been telling a few of my clients I'm getting my dick sucked."

TJ snickered and Bruno glared at him.

"While I appreciate honesty in a hacker, I would prefer a little more professionalism."

"Then you shoulda hired some gum-popping tween." TJ stood up. "The Meredith, Baxter, and Turner cases." He snapped checks and invoices down as he spoke. "And the Kramer case." He placed a DVD box, along with another check and invoice on the desk. "Are all closed with tearful and grateful thanks."

Bruno gaped as he examined each check. "These are for more than we agreed upon."

TJ dropped back into his chair. "I renegotiated your fee as well as your expenses to reflect a more comparable rate with your competitors."

"TJ..."

"No need to thank me. I will be collecting my normal fee along with a ten percent raise."

Bruno nodded then went to the door with "Big Baby Investigations" etched on the glass. "Could you not tell clients about my sex life?"

"Then don't leave me to hold down the office for weeks on end." TJ turned back to his monitors and was soon engrossed in his work. The phone ringing invaded, but he pushed the noise aside as a window opened on the monitor he used for Cailyn's computer. He'd been keeping track of the files that were being monitored. Now those same files were being altered further. He turned the volume down and watched the date unfold. He gave a low whistle then reached for his phone.

"God dammit, TJ!" Bruno stepped to the door of his office. "That was my contact at the station. Avery is dead."

TJ stared at him a moment. Why did that name sound familiar. TJ paced the office, chewing on one end of a dreadlock. Avery? Avery.

"Did you hear me?"

TJ threw up a hand to silence Red. When he did, he swore. "Fuck a duck with a dildo. Lasko Entertainment."

Red sighed. "Is that the company I told you to file?"

He nodded, flopped into his rolling chair, and shoved off until he was in front of his keyboard. "Yeah. I've got more info on them now, and oh shit, she's in serious trouble."

"Who? What broad? What business?"

"A favor for the kink bros."

Red grunted. "I thought I told you to leave them alone."

"Man, they needed a favor, and you know I can't resist a D-i-D." TJ kept his attention on the screens while his thin fingers flew across the keys. Data flitted across the screens so fast, Red wasn't sure how the other man kept up with it. "When did he die?"

"Tonight. Was murdered during a break-in."

TJ stopped typing. "At his home?"

"That's all the information I got: was that it was during a break-in. I don't think it was his crib though."

TJ resumed typing. Before his walk on the gray side of the law, he used to write software and even held a regular nine-to-five working cybersecurity for some of the largest companies. He made good money, but he much preferred what he was doing now: not-so-ethical hacking.

"I've been looking into this and a few other companies. I need to let them know what's going on."

Red's bulk pressed in behind as he peered over TJ's shoulder. "That's a lot of zeroes in those accounts."

"Yeah." He pointed to a pending transaction on another screen. "See this? This transfer was initiated ten minutes ago. Somebody other than our Mr. Avery is trying to move some money around. Should I block it or let it go through?"

"Let it go through. I wanna see where the money goes."

"And I'll let the kink bros know there's movement on the money."

Roman could barely contain his excitement. He had Cailyn all to himself this evening and had the perfect ensemble he wanted to see on her luscious curves. He hung the pink striped bag on the door to the bathroom then settled on one corner of the king-size bed. He checked the supply of condoms. Next to the condoms were a pair of padded handcuffs and a bottle of coconut oil.

He liked the oil, not just for the scent but for the versatility. As a lubricant it lasted much longer than any other he'd used, and it didn't get tacky or eat through condoms.

His gaze lingered on the handcuffs. Would she be game for a little bondage? Sure they'd hinted and flirted about it over dinner, but hinting and flirting were far from doing. The door to the bathroom opened and his jaw dropped. The pale blue nightie hit her just below the curve of her buttocks. The deep plunge of the spaghetti strap bodice cinched below her modest bust and thrust her breasts upward. The tiny triangle of silk hinted at a shaved vagina.

"I take it you don't like the outfit," she teased.

He laughed. "You are so sassy."

She moved forward until she was just within reach. The soft scent of pear and jasmine enveloped him and he inhaled appreciatively.

"That's what I do." She stepped back as he rose.

Roman placed his hands on her waist and stared into her eyes. "I'm a demanding lover and sometimes a little rough," he began. He inched the hem upward. "I'll do my best not to leave a mark on your skin." He dropped a kiss to the curve of her shoulder, nipped at the sensitive skin, then eased it with a swirl of his tongue.

He caressed the bare skin above the waistband of the thong and she trembled in his arms. "If I do anything you don't like, tell me," he murmured in her ear. "I want our time together to be as pleasurable for you as it is for me."

She settled her hands at the waistband of his slacks. "So are you planning to use the cuffs or not?" She ran deft fingers over the outline of his erection through his pants.

Before she could blink, he had her on the bed and cuffed to the headboard. She giggled. "Damn."

He flashed a wicked grin then feasted on the sight of her splayed on his bed. From his vantage point, he could see the crotch of her thong was already damp and she was definitely neat and trimmed. Just a hint of pubic hair was visible beneath the material. He allowed his gaze to wander upward over her lush thighs and hips. Her soft belly and those delectable breasts. He took in her full bottom lip and slumberous eyes. Heat and desire ignited his own.

How many nights had he dreamed of having her just like this? Of seeing her in his bed in just this outfit? Ready for him? He slowly stripped, the desire in her irises darkening. A small thrill rippled through him at the intensity of her gaze. He allowed his trousers and underwear to fall to the floor and his shirt followed. He stroked his hard length and watched her eyes widen at the sight of him.

Yeah, he was proud of his dick. It was long, thick, and he definitely knew how to use it. He knelt on the bed and then reached for a condom. He didn't want to forget in the heat of passion. When he wanted to take her, he didn't want to have to stop to grab protection.

He kissed her. Soft and sensuous, before deepening the kiss. She tasted like fresh pears, and he couldn't get enough of her. He allowed his hands to rove over her, tweaking the hard buds of her nipples. She moaned and writhed next to him. He loved how she was just giving herself to him. He pinched her nipples again and she moaned into his mouth, arching her back for more. He obliged.

Roman left her mouth to sample one taut peak while he pushed aside the damp triangle of fabric to find her slick and hot. He circled her little pearl while he sucked hard on her nipple. She rewarded him with more of her damp heat. He plunged a long finger inside her. She was so slick and hot, he added a second finger and slowly moved them in and out. Her walls clenched on his fingers and his cock leapt in response.

"When I take you, it'll be hard, fast, and you'll feel every inch of me," he murmured. Her hips were riding his hand.

He added additional pressure to her clit and she fell apart. He watched her go to pieces with all the male satisfaction he could muster.

Roman nudged her legs apart, not allowing her to come down from the orgasm before he slowly entered her. She was so tight and hot, it was as if he wore no protection at all. Her vagina pulsed around him. He withdrew and then buried balls deep once more. She tossed her head back, moaning his name.

He grasped her ankles, spreading her legs wide as he stroked hard and fast. She clenched her fists, pulling against the cuffs as he thrust into her, applying friction to her little pearl, feeling the ripple of her sex as it spasmed once again.

Sweat rolled down his face and back. He slowed his pace enough to place her legs over his arms and grasped her buttocks. Each downward stroke kept his pelvis in constant contact with hers. There was no way she could move and not feel every inch of him.

He was intense and all-consuming. Never in her wildest dreams did she think it could be like this. And the added bonus of being bound while he ravaged her? There was no other word for it. She was a quivering, pulsating mass of nerves for him. Two orgasms and she was fastly sliding to her third. She didn't think it was possible.

"Please, Roman. I can't."

A throaty chuckle was her answer as he proved her wrong. His shout joined hers. He collapsed over her, their bodies still locked in the intimate embrace. Slowly he withdrew, her body protesting, gripping at his semihard dick.

Through half-closed lids, she watched him pad to the bathroom. The water ran, and then a moment later, he returned with a towel. Before she could protest, he gently cleaned her then dropped the towel on the bedside table.

Only then did he release the cuffs and gather her in his arms.

He trailed lazy circles over her skin. "Was I too rough on you?"

She shook her head, her body still reeling from their lovemaking. "I had no idea."

He brushed damp hair from her forehead. "We're not done yet. That was just a preview."

She wiggled in his arms until she straddled him. He nudged her bottom up and used the sheet as a barrier. She merely smiled. "Just a preview?"

"Oh yes. We have the whole night."

Buzzing permeated his sleep. Israel moaned as he reached for his phone. He nearly jerked the charger from the wall before his addled brain realized what he was doing.

"This better be good," he slurred into the phone. Turning his head, he buried his face in the pillow. It smelled faintly of pears and jasmine. Cailyn's scent.

"The money is on the move," TJ said without preamble.

"People are trying to sleep." He sniffed deeper. If he hadn't been such a jackass last night, Cailyn could've been beside him, warm and wet. His body stirred at the hint of desire.

"And Avery is dead."

Well that dampened the mood. With great effort, Israel sat up. He shouldn't have had so much to drink last night, but how else was he going to make it through the night when he knew for certain Cailyn was spending the night in Roman's bed?

Of course she'd spend the night with Roman. It wasn't as if Israel had given her a choice. He'd practically shoved her at Roman with his temper and such. Israel knew exactly how Roman would seduce her. How many times had they shared a woman? Even now his penis throbbed at the thought of sharing Cailyn with Roman.

And he knew Cailyn would be open and willing. After all, she had approached him. And if he could be honest, he missed the energy of the threesomes. He could imagine Cailyn begging for release, spread-eagle and wet for him. Maybe even sucking Roman off.

Israel shook his head. No sense in torturing himself with fantasies.

"You're fucking up a perfectly good hangover right now," Israel murmured.

"Bro, get you head out your ass and hear what I'm saying," TJ snapped. "One of the companies that your lady brought to me is in play. Someone offed the accountholder and is now moving the money."

That sobered Israel. "All right. Tell me what you've got."

TJ quickly launched into what he'd learned about the Lasko account and the death of Avery.

"I know Avery's dead. I saw his body at the morgue. Someone worked him over pretty good before they killed him." Israel stumbled from the bed on a desperate search for some aspirin. He found two and downed them with half a bottle of water. The plastic crinkled as he emptied it. He went in search for more.

"Whoever this guy is is good. I mean really good," TJ was saying. "It's all I can do to keep up with him."

"Can you see where the money is going?" He found a cold bottle in the mini-fridge, twisted off the cap, and drank.

"Oh yeah." Keys tapping flowed through the line. "Look. The money's moving again and I need to concentrate. Let your boy know the money is moving again. He hasn't hit me back since I told him."

Israel ground his teeth. He should've known Roman would've dragged TJ into this. Pressing the bottle to his forehead, all the tension left his body. How could he be mad when he'd taken the same steps to help Cailyn? "Yeah. I'll do that."

Paul stared at the screen on his phone. Anything of any value to him, including his laptop, sat in the oversized backpack at his feet. He'd tried rather unsuccessfully to reach Cailyn at the firm, and he was more than worried. He glanced around the crowded courtyard.

Various outdoor tables dotted the perimeter of the courtyard. Snatches of conversations wafted toward him while the mingling scents of pizza, coffee, and sugar wafted on the air.

He stiffened as a shadow passed over him, then the owner dropped into the chair opposite. "You are a very hard man to find," the newcomer said.

Paul made a move to stand. The man shot out a hand and grabbed his wrist, preventing him from moving without causing a scene. He studied the tall Black man seated across from him.

Short-cropped hair, almost bald on the sides, and a somewhat hard edge to the half-smile twisting the wide mouth. The man wore a crisp, bright blue dress shirt, red striped tie, and a tweed jacket. When the man shifted, Paul caught a glimpse of a holstered gun.

"We have a mutual friend." With his free hand, the man pushed a business card across the table.

Paul glanced at it and gasped. Police. How much did she know? Had she figured out who was behind the hinky accounts? His heart beat a little faster. "Is she okay? I've tried calling her at the office and…"

"She's fine." The man moved his hand, satisfied Paul wasn't going to bolt. "I'm a cop. Detective Dagon." Roman slowly removed his badge and palmed it for Paul to see. "Cailyn sent me to find you."

He slumped in the chair, but his pulse still raced. "I was so worried. My place was ransacked, so I grabbed what I needed and have been staying with friends."

"I noticed that when I went by your place."

What information could he get from this officer without seeming to do so? Would he tell him about Cailyn's apartment? And how did he maneuver the conversation to what he wanted? "Sir, this isn't something I signed up for." Paul shook his head. "This is insane. I'm just an intern. I can't do anything without supervision, and people are trying to find me. What the hell is going on?"

Roman scanned the faces of the crowd. "You and Cailyn stumbled onto something you weren't supposed to. You both have seen something you weren't supposed to see and now they want to keep you both silent." His gaze lingered on a figure who kept his face hidden, but the body language said he was paying attention to them. "Let me take you to Cailyn. She's gonna be really happy to see you."

"You mean those accounts weren't legit?" He pushed back his chair, reaching for his bag. Tension from the other man had him glancing around. Nothing stood out. There were the same people as earlier, families eating, teenagers laughing and joking. Nothing that screamed danger.

"Does anyone know you're meeting me?" Roman never stopped scanning the crowd, but his gaze continued to return to the starer.

"Yes." Paul flashed a wry smile. "I told them where I would be just in case I went missing."

Roman nodded. "Okay. Did you bring a friend with you?" He leaned forward, using the movement to mask he was slipping his hand in to unsnap the weapon holster.

"No." For the first time, unease tightened Paul's gut. Had they come for him? "We have a prearranged signal."

Roman met the younger man's gaze. "Listen to me very carefully. Do exactly what I tell you and I'll get you to Cailyn."

Fear filled Paul's eyes, but he nodded. *Well, shit.* What had he done to bring this type of heat? "All right."

"I drive a black Nissan Maxima." Roman slid him the keys. "Parked on the southside of the building behind me, third row, fourth one in."

Paul stood, clutching his backpack to his chest. "Black Maxima?"

"Yes. You'll be fine."

Nodding, Paul hurried past Roman. Roman observed that the other man turned to follow. Roman placed himself between Paul and the other man. Roman hurried forward, bumping the man as he went.

"Watch where the fuck you're going." The man shoved Roman aside.

Roman used the momentum to knock the man further off-balance as he lifted his wallet. "Sorry, man. Tripped over the chair." He chanced a glance over his shoulder. Paul had disappeared into the crowd.

The man walked off in a huff. Roman hurried around the corner and to his vehicle. Paul was just getting into the passenger side when the first shot rang out. Screams echoed off the buildings. Paul dove into the car even as the passenger window on the car next to him shattered. Glass flew like tiny diamonds.

Roman had his weapon in his hand before he realized what he was doing. He scanned the crowd for the shooter. Another shot rang out as those who hadn't found cover flattened themselves to the pavement. There, just to his left. The man he'd seen staring at Paul. The same man he'd bumped and lifted his wallet.

"Police! Drop your weapon!" Roman bellowed raising his own weapon.

The man swung in his direction and fired off two rounds. Roman dove. He couldn't risk firing, there were too many civilians between them. Bullets whizzed by his head, one so close he felt the heat singe his ear. It ricocheted off the building behind him. Cement cut the side of his neck just above the collar of his shirt. He winced and aimed. *Damn!* He still didn't have a clear shot.

Sirens blared in the distance. The man waved at Roman, turned, and fled. Roman managed a smirk. He still had the man's wallet.

Erring on the side of caution, Cailyn worked from home. Well not her home, per se, but Roman's. Her home was still considered a crime scene. She eyed the two large suitcases standing in the foyer. The detective in charge had been kind enough to allow Roman to grab her some clothes. Since she had no idea how long her apartment would be considered a crime scene, he'd grabbed everything he could stuff into the luggage.

And he still hadn't let her see what her bedroom looked like.

How had they gotten into her apartment? That's what bothered her the most. Someone had to have known where she lived and what they were looking for. Pursing her lips, she leaned back in the chair. Unable to settle, she stood and stretched.

Her spine popped as she reached for the ceiling.

She breathed in and out, letting her mind clear so she could replay the last few days. Something had been said the other night that stuck in her brain. Something about one of the interns. She walked into the kitchen, filling the electric kettle with water before searching through the cabinets for tea. What had the man said? *He couldn't be ham-fisted. Don't you know who the intern is? Why worry about the intern?*

The kettle clicked off and she poured boiling water over the bag in her mug. Carefully she carried the mug back to the table. She resumed her seat then typed in the website of her company. They hadn't updated the site yet and she clicked on the "About Us" tab. There she found thumbnails of all the partners and employees.

The company had been in a bit of an uproar with Barry Johnson's death. His death was the reason why all the accounts were being audited. It was standard operating procedure for their firm. If someone died or went on vacation, accounts were double-checked. In another month, they would have an independent auditor come in, but for now, she was doing her job.

She clicked on Barry's name. His bio with the date of his death filled her screen. A small obituary was there as well. She read through the family section. He'd left behind a loving, devoted wife, daughters Abigail and Alexa, and two sons Jacob and Peter. There was a family photo that was at least ten years old. She clicked on that. It showed the family standing in front of a Christmas tree. The kids had to be in their teens. She enlarged the photo. There was something familiar about Jacob. She'd seen him before. But where?

She backtracked, now studying the rest of the partners. Bridget Lockwood and Roy LaMont were the founding partners. The newest, Carter Stanley, bought in shortly after Johnson's death. She clicked on his bio. It didn't show he was married, but did list him as an attentive father. The man was not always the most ethical person, and she didn't know why the founding partners would want his name on the letterhead. Stanley tried to cut corners whenever possible.

In the early days when they were both lowly accountants, she had known him as a fierce competitor. But as he advanced in the company and brought in larger accounts, some of his practices skated on the barely legal side. If there was a loophole to be exploited, Stanley would make it squeak.

And he was the one who told her to leave off the discrepancies in the accounts.

Thoughtfully, she sipped her tea. Exploiting loopholes wasn't a far step from inflating or deflating balance sheets for better loan terms and definitely not out of the realm for embezzling. But would the man jeopardize his license and career for money? This was something she should bounce off of Israel or Roman, or both. She glanced at her watch. Should she give Roman a call? He did say he was going to look for Paul again. Maybe she should check on Israel. She picked up her phone and tapped his name.

The phone rang three times before it clicked over to voicemail. "Hey. Just checking on you. Give me a call, please. I love you." She disconnected. What was she going to do?

She covered her face with her hands before dragging her fingers through her hair. This wouldn't be the first time her lifestyle choice caused friction. She almost snorted a laugh. Friction was such a kind word. Growing up she'd always known she was a little different. Her parents were swingers. That's not what they called it. She'd just thought they were fun parties where the grown-ups got to swap keys. That and the upside-down pineapple.

She wasn't into casual sex like that, but rather preferred the intimacy of a relationship. And yes, she preferred to be in the middle of two men. Right now she wanted the certainty of Roman and Israel.

Both men were attentive and caring. Israel was more in touch with his feelings and a bit more insecure, but she figured that had to do with the scar on his face. Personally she adored the scar and it added to the attractiveness of his face. Then, of course, there was the hair. He had the softest afro she had the pleasure of sinking her fingers into.

But Roman had scars too. She'd seen the thin line bisecting his throat. But where Israel was unsure of his place, Roman knew exactly who and what he was to her. Roman embraced her lifestyle and even wanted a threesome.

Could they make it more?

What would it feel like to be sandwiched between the two men she loved most? To have their hands running over her body, caressing and tasting? She shifted as heat throbbed between her legs. Or she'd love the opportunity to suck them both off. Her breath hitched. Could she make them cum at the same time?

Well enough of that. Sitting there fantasizing about her men was not going to get her any closer to answers. If anything, it would get her closer to frustration, a cold shower, or having to masturbate. And she'd much rather have the real thing.

Cailyn pushed her half-empty mug away from her laptop then pulled the files closer. At least numbers made sense. The math didn't lie. She could lose herself in spreadsheets, profit and loss statements, balance sheets. Those she could put in order. Love, unfortunately, could not be computed the same way.

She might not be able to neatly arrange her love life, but she could do her best to unravel how the money was being transferred out. All she needed was a sliver of a thread.

Keys rattling broke through the calm of working. Cailyn blinked bleary eyes to bring her watch into focus. She'd been at this for hours.

Standing, she stretched the kinks from her muscles and groaned as her joints popped and protested the move. Her arms were over her head when Roman came into view.

"Hey."

The smile and greeting died on her lips as she took in his disheveled appearance. Slowly she lowered her arms as she stared at the bandage on the side of his neck. To her utter horror, dried blood marred his collar and trailed down the front of his shirt.

"What happened?" Cailyn hurried to him but stopped just outside of his reach. She lifted a hand to touch him but was afraid to.

As if sensing her distress, Roman grasped her fingers and drew her into a one-armed hug. "I'm fine. Flying shrapnel cut me."

Cailyn held him close, breathing in his scent. This close she also got a whiff of antiseptic, the coppery taint of blood, and of all things, fried rice. A bag rattled at her back.

"But what happened?" She pulled back enough to view his face then let her fingers drift over the bandage.

"I found Paul." Roman turned so the young man could precede him into the hall.

"Oh, thank God!" She released Roman and hugged Paul. "I've been absolutely frantic over you. Where have you been?"

He returned her hug then disentangled from her. His eyes were wide and a bit unfocused as he looked from her to Roman and back again. "With friends," he answered. "Ms. Finch, what's going on?"

"I'm not entirely sure." She led him to the living room.

Roman closed the door. "I brought dinner." He held up the paper bag. "I didn't feel like cooking."

"What happened?" she insisted, settling into the leather sofa.

"He saved my life." Paul plopped into the matching chair. He placed trembling hands between his knees. "Someone started shooting, and oh God. Do you have something to drink? And not water?"

"I've just the thing." Roman moved past them, set the bag on the coffee table, then continued to a small cabinet. He opened it, pulling out a bottle of Glenfiddich. He poured three fingers worth in three glasses and then passed them out.

Paul gulped his down then coughed. Roman eyed him over the rim of his glass. "Want another?"

Paul nodded and held out his glass. Roman refilled it.

"Sit down and eat something." Roman knocked back the rest of his whiskey then refilled his glass. He glanced at Cailyn. "Baby girl, I will tell you everything. I just need to settle my nerves a bit."

"Other than the blood, are you okay?"

He nodded then crooked a finger at her. She stood in front of him. With his free hand, he tilted her face upward and then crushed his mouth to hers. For a moment, Cailyn could only feel. All the fear, excitement, weariness, and love flowed through that one demanding kiss.

She clung to him, savoring the taste of him mingling with the aged alcohol. Tears pricked her eyes at the depth of emotion his kiss invoked. She did love him, just as fiercely as she loved Israel, and on some level, she knew she could've lost Roman today.

"I'm so sorry," she murmured against his lips.

He chuckled. "For what?"

"Dragging you into my mess."

He kissed her again, his hand moving down her butt to usher her closer. A throat clearing behind them reminded them they weren't alone. "Damn, I forgot we had a houseguest."

She giggled. "Right." Reluctantly she left the warmth of his body then moved into the kitchen for plates and silverware.

Roman retrieved the bag from the coffee table and carried it to the counter. He unpacked cartons of Chinese food. "I got a little bit of everything. Mu shu, sweet and sour, beef and broccoli. There's a carton of spicy prawns, so be careful."

"I swear this is amateur hour," Roman said between bites of egg roll and fried rice. They sat around the island with plates of food. "After I sent Paul to the car, I lifted the guy's wallet. I had no idea the moron was going to start shooting."

Cailyn drank what remained of her whiskey, the alcohol warming her from the inside out. "We've got to go to the police with this or at least someone who can understand what's going on."

Roman covered her hand with his and gave it a gentle squeeze. "The two of you are perfectly safe here. The police are stepping up patrols, and I called in a favor to a buddy of mine who runs a security firm. He's got a couple of guys stationed in and around the area."

Paul stared at his plate. "What did we find?"

Cailyn dabbed her napkin to the corners of her mouth. "We found proof of embezzlement."

CHAPTER EIGHT

"**A** shoot-out with the police!" Stanley roared. "Have you lost your mind?"

Harold Murray winced. "What was I supposed to do?"

"There is footage of the incident for all the world to see. Anybody with a cellphone captured your assassination attempt. One person even streamed it live on their social media platforms!" Stanley rounded on the smaller man. "I'm this close to leaving the firm with hundreds of millions of dollars, and you're headlining on CNN!"

"That's not the worst of it. I lost my wallet."

Black rage filled the silence. The tension snapped and crackled like a live wire. Stanley picked up a vase and hurled it mere inches from Murray's head. "I'd kill you myself, but that will only lead back to me faster."

Murray blanched.

"Get the fuck outta my sight and don't contact me until I give you the all clear."

Murray nodded and disappeared from the office. Stanley didn't need this.

With a sigh, he dropped into his chair. How could his operation go so wrong? First, Avery up and disappears, totally leaving him in a lurch. That damn Cailyn Finch and her thoroughness. He thought he could corrupt her, but somehow he'd read her wrong. She was one of those ethical accountants who had a rigid outlook on what should be done with a firm's finances as long as it complied with the law.

Well what about the law of robbing the rich so he could get richer? Hell, that's what his ex-wives had done. He would just have to move up his timeline. He sat behind his desk, waking his computer by shaking the mouse.

He verified the amount of money he had ready for deposit and smiled in satisfaction. He typed a few keys, checking the other amounts. Satisfied, he picked up the phone and dialed a number. As much as he'd like to take the rest of the money, he knew when it was time to cut his losses and move on. It was time for him to disappear.

"Someone shot you!" Cailyn knocked Roman's hands aside as she inspected his wound. They were alone in his room. Paul was safely ensconced in the guest bedroom, sound asleep thanks to food and alcohol.

Roman chuckled as Cailyn swatted his hand away again. He had long since showered away the dried blood, with Cailyn's help, and now he lay in the bed, naked except for the sheet to his waist. Cailyn straddled him, wearing only one of his t-shirts.

Finally he succeeded in capturing her wrists. He held them close to his chest. "I was grazed, and it was flying debris that caused the scratch."

She jerked at his hold on her wrists but was unsuccessful in freeing herself. Instead he held her in one strong hand while his free arm pulled her next to him into the haven of his body. He sighed. Instinctively his body curled around hers. He needed this contact. It reminded him he was alive. "You were bleeding!" she protested.

He released her to hold her tightly in his arms. "Yes, and a lot more people could've been hurt." He held her gaze. "I came home to you. I will always come home to you."

She blinked back tears. "You can't make that promise when someone may shoot at you again."

He brushed her tears away. "We've just begun our adventure together, Cailyn. I'm not going to get careless now."

She managed a watery chuckle. "You've never been careless."

"Then you know I will always come home to you."

They fell silent. Muted pulsing of subwoofers cranked up, bounced through the ceiling. Cailyn glanced upward. "Sounds like they're having a good time."

"Yeah, they'll turn it down around midnight." Roman stroked her arm then flashed a wicked grin. "They know there's a cop in the building."

She giggled. "No wonder things have gotten quieter on this floor."

"The building manager caught me on my way out the other day and said she uses the phrase 'in-house cop' to deter some of the more questionable applicants."

"I know I appreciate you being right down the hall. There's no way I'd have stayed calm if you weren't around."

He stroked her hair before brushing a kiss across her temple. "Baby girl, I will protect you with my dying breath."

The phone ringing broke the gravity of the declaration. Roman eased his arm from beneath Cailyn then grabbed his phone. "Roman."

"Money is on the move," TJ said without preamble.

"Where?" Roman tapped Cailyn. "Someone's going after the money."

Cailyn widened her eyes. "So soon?"

"Ahh, no wonder Israel found his way down the bottom of a bottle."

"Well he better find his way out if he wants a piece of this action," Roman quipped. "Where's the cash going?"

"Where would you like me to send it?" TJ said, a wide smile in his voice.

"Uh huh. That's what I thought."

The braying laugh filtered through the line. "That's what I like about you man, you know when not to say nothing."

"How long ago did you tell Rael?"

Heavy pounding on the door vibrated the air.

"I'll get it." Cailyn tossed the sheets aside, swung her legs out the bed, then stood. The t-shirt settled into place, the hem just covering the curve of her bottom.

"Thanks, TJ." Roman disconnected the call. "Put some clothes on first or he's liable to go ballistic again."

"Bra and panties too?" She tossed a wicked smile over her shoulder.

He groaned. "I'd like to think of you without those." He nodded as if coming to a decision. "No. Just the t-shirt and your skirt."

She stifled a laugh. "You're mean when you want to be."

"And don't you forget it."

Cailyn checked the peephole then threw back the locks. She managed a slight squeak when the door pushed in. She saved her bare toes from being scraped—barely. She glared at Israel, who looked sheepish.

"I'm sorry."

She looked him up and down. Bloodshot eyes, rumpled clothes, and his shoes were untied. "I'll make coffee." She turned on her heel without waiting to see if he'd follow.

"Dammit, Cailyn."

She swung around with fire in her eyes. "Dammit, Rael!" Her tone exasperated.

He stalked toward her, lust and something else snapping in his eyes. She fisted her hands on her hips, lifting her chin in defiance.

He grabbed her by the shoulders, hauled her against his body, and crushed his mouth to hers. The kiss threw her. He tasted of mint and the faintest hint of whiskey. When he released her, she stumbled back against another solid wall of muscle. The beginnings of her fantasy. She was between the two men she loved most.

"That's not an apology," she stated a bit breathlessly, grateful for Roman's strength behind her.

"No, it's not, but it's a start." Israel allowed his gaze to hold hers then shifted to look above her head. "I'm here because of Cailyn. We can set aside our differences for her."

Roman inclined his head. "And when this is over, we're going to sit down and talk."

Israel clenched his jaw.

Cailyn stepped from between the two men. "I'm making coffee."

"I don't drink coffee," Israel told her.

"You do tonight," she said without turning around.

"I have really pissed her off," Israel muttered.

"Yep." Roman couldn't quite keep the amusement from his voice.

Israel narrowed his eyes. "You don't have to sound so smug."

Roman lifted one shoulder in a careless shrug. He looked over his old friend. "You look like you've had a bad night."

"Was working my way through a hangover." Israel shuffled to a nearby chair and plopped into the oversize cushions with a sigh of relief. He dropped his head in his hands. "I fucked that up too."

The scent of rich, fragrant coffee filled the air. It was followed by the clink and clatter of dishes on glass.

Roman studied the bent form in front of him. "I don't blame you for what happened when we were partners. I never did," he began quietly. "If anything, I was more hurt that you left me to deal with the squad by myself."

Israel looked up quickly just as Cailyn appeared with a tray of cups and coffee.

"Here, let me help you with that." Roman hurried to her and relieved her of the tray.

She crossed the room and took the chair opposite Israel. The only other seating was the other end of the sofa he occupied. Roman cast her a curious glance.

She flashed him a coy smile as she tucked her legs beneath her, but not before he saw a flash of skin beneath her skirt. He stifled a laugh as Israel groaned.

"Well played, Cailyn." Roman offered her a short salute.

"Do you plan to torture me the entire time I'm here?" Israel muttered. "Believe me, between knowing I'm an ass and this hangover, I'm suffering."

Wordlessly Cailyn held out her hand. In her open palm was a bottle of pain relievers.

Israel brushed her hand as his fingers closed over the bottle. "I'm sorry, sweetheart," he said. "I was wrong to take my temper out on you."

The sincerity in his voice melted the rest of her resolve. She held his gaze for a moment and then nodded. "Okay."

Roman set a thick mug on the table at Israel's elbow, while Roman took his cup of coffee and sat on the other end of the sofa.

Israel checked his watch, not sure if he should mix the aspirin he'd taken early with this. Instead, he read the label and erring on the side of caution opened the bottle, shook a tablet in hand, then grimaced at the mug on the side table. He popped the pills in his mouth then chased it with the hot liquid. He swallowed and stared at Cailyn. Gratitude and something else shone through.

"You're welcome," she said. She held his gaze a moment longer then looked at Roman. "So what are the two of you going to do to keep me and my assistant safe?"

CHAPTER NINE

"What assistant?" Israel demanded. He set the mug down so hard, amber liquid sloshed over the rim. Cursing, he picked up the mug and wiped away the moisture with his sleeve.

"The one who's sleeping in my spare room." Roman sipped his coffee. "Perfect." He nudged a coaster toward Israel.

Mumbling, he set the mug on the surface protector. Israel scrubbed the heel of his hand over his face. "I really am out of the loop."

"And someone took a shot at me, or rather, her assistant."

Israel stood. "Pack a bag, Cailyn, you're going somewhere safe." He'd taken two steps and circled Cailyn's wrist. She didn't pull away as he expected but slipped her hand into his.

She stared up at him. Waiting.

"She's safe where she is," Roman said quietly.

Israel swung his gaze to Roman. Emotion trembled down his arm and tightened his hand on Cailyn's. She caressed his knuckles with her thumb. The motion cleared some of the fog from his brain. "Safe? Someone from her firm was murdered in her apartment. Down the hall from your 'very safe' residence." He couldn't quite keep the sarcasm from his voice.

With great deliberation, Roman set his mug down with a quiet snap. "Take your head outta your ass long enough to look at my setup." Roman stretched out his legs then crossed his bare feet at the ankles. "The only reason you got to this floor and my apartment is because security has you on the list."

"Security? That fat, 'tard downstairs..." Finally, Israel released Cailyn and plopped back on the sofa as he recalled the bum sitting on the outside stoop and then the maintenance worker changing light bulbs in the downstairs lobby. "You called in help."

Roman nodded. "I love her too and have no desire to see her harmed."

At that, Cailyn stood and took the unoccupied cushion between the two men. She stretched out with her feet in Roman's lap and settled into Israel's arms.

For a moment no one spoke. Israel leaned over and buried his nose in her hair, taking her scent of jasmine and pears deep into his lungs.

He closed his eyes, savoring her. The warmth of her body, the softness of her hair splayed over his lap. The way her lashes fringed her eyes. How her mouth dipped and pulled, the way her bottom lip was fuller than the top. His gaze drifted lower. The outline of her nipples, dark and erect, pushed against the white cotton of the t-shirt.

Roman's t-shirt. For some reason that didn't bother him, and maybe it should have. She wore her skirt, but her little display earlier let him know nothing else was beneath the garment.

Her feet, the toenails painted a neon blue, were cradled in Roman's lap. This seemed completely natural. Not a shred of tension was in her body. If anything, Cailyn was completely relaxed between the two of them. He found he wanted her relaxed.

If he closed his eyes, he could forget the tension between him and Roman. Forget the chasm separating them. If he stayed in the present, in the now, he could pretend it was old times. Pretend they were in love with the same woman and would pleasure her without artifice. But they were in love with the same woman. Roman even proposed a threesome before he'd known Israel was the other man in her life. And he was still willing to share Cailyn with Israel.

But was Israel willing to share Cailyn with Roman?

Gently, Israel traced the outline of Cailyn's lips. She kissed his fingertip. Pleasure shivered through his body. Sitting there with her bridging the both of them, Israel let his body sag. What he tried to achieve with alcohol and temper now swept over him. Peace. And a sense of belonging. For the first time in years, he found his place again. But he couldn't have this with Roman. Or could he?

He glanced up to find Roman studying him. He managed to muster up a scowl and looked away.

What had Roman seen? Had he seen the longing? Would he use it against him?

"So what happens now?" Cailyn snuggled between the two men.

Israel focused on the present.

"We wait and see where the money goes." Roman rubbed her feet with one hand, while he drained the remainder of his coffee with the other.

"I think I made some progress on how the money was skimmed from the accounts without anyone knowing." She covered a wide yawn. "They didn't follow procedures when one of the partners, Barry Johnson, died suddenly." Without opening her eyes, she offered a small smile. "I have to admit, the two of you are bringing my fantasies to life right now." She wiggled her toes. "That feels so good."

"Your fantasy is to have one man rub your feet while another runs his fingers through your hair?" Israel fluttered a kiss over her mouth.

"Absolutely."

"We could do so much more than this." Roman's voice was pure temptation. He slid a hand up her calf as he held Israel's gaze.

Was this a challenge? Israel didn't look away. He allowed one palm to settle over Cailyn's breast. Just that small movement caused her breath to hitch. She arched into his hand. Absently, he circled her nipple with his thumb.

"This could be like old times," Roman stated, inching his fingers up higher, bunching Cailyn's skirt as he went. Before she could shift, he trailed his hand back down to massage her feet. He didn't tug her skirt down.

Israel stared at the exposed expanse of thigh. A little higher, and her delightful pussy would be on full display. Was he ready for this? His body was if his throbbing cock was any indication. But could he handle the emotional output?

Cailyn reached up and touched his cheek.

"I want you," he admitted. "I want to fulfill your fantasy…"

"But not tonight," she finished for him.

He looked away unable to bear her condemnation. Gentle pressure on his chin forced him to look at her again. There was nothing but love and understanding in her eyes. Somehow that was worse.

"This is a good start." She lifted enough to brush her lips to his. "Thank you."

He kissed her again, cradling the back of her head in his palm. "I don't deserve you," he murmured.

"But I love you anyway," she assured him.

A long moment passed before anyone spoke again. Israel basked in the warmth of not only Cailyn's love, but her acceptance. For giving him time to come to terms with the changing relationship dynamic. He studied Roman in his periphery. Yes, the relationship was changing. Roman still rubbed Cailyn's feet, but now her skirt was smoothed down. When had that happened?

"Will TJ be able to follow the money back to its source?" Cailyn asked.

"In his sleep," Roman assured her.

"Has Red made it back?" Israel smoothed Cailyn's hair from her face.

"Yeah. They were both in the office when he called. I could hear Red barking orders in the background," Roman responded.

Israel stared into Cailyn's face. The sooty fringe of her lashes rested on her cheeks while her full lips seemed to smile at some inner secret. Only her deep, even breathing gave away that she'd fallen asleep.

"I had no clue she was dating you," Roman said after a long while.

"She told me that after I swung at you." Israel sighed. "I can't lose her, Roman."

"Neither can I," Roman agreed.

"Had I known things would be this dangerous, I wouldn't have agreed to help her." He grimaced as he realized how his words sounded. "I didn't mean it like that."

"I know what you meant. We both would've gone about this a different way. Neither of us wants her hurt." Roman lifted Cailyn's feet from his lap and set them gently on the sofa. She didn't even stir. He stood, clearing the empty mugs. "If we hadn't helped her, she'd have found a way to do it." He left the living room and returned a short time later. "Take Cailyn to bed, I'll bunk out here tonight."

Israel winged a brow. "What?" He fully expected to be the one bunking on the couch. Alone. Not in the bed with Cailyn.

Roman grinned. "I'm being the gentleman. Take my room for the rest of the night. Get some sleep."

Roman shook his head as Israel continued to stare at him, mouth agape. Roman crossed the room and lifted Cailyn as if she weighed nothing. "Follow me, lover boy."

Dumbly Israel followed Roman down the short hall and into a spacious master bedroom. The bedsheets were mussed, and for a moment, a flare of jealousy fizzled, but what surprised him most was the pang of regret.

In another time and place, he and Roman would've shared the bed with Cailyn.

"I don't feel right about kicking you out of your room," he began lamely.

Roman laid Cailyn near the center of the king-size bed. For a moment his fingers lingered on the curve of her cheek before he straightened and pulled the covers to her chin.

For one moment, love, stark and deep, transformed Roman's features into something so intimate, Israel had to look away. He couldn't, in good conscience, allow his insecurities to sabotage something so pure.

"You could sleep on the other side of her."

Roman straightened. "It's late, Rael. I don't want this to be another fight between us."

He hung his head. "Just for tonight." He searched for the right words. "Just for tonight, I need it to be like we're still friends."

For a long moment, Roman studied Israel. Wordlessly he sat on the edge of the bed. "Close the door." He pulled off his pajama bottoms and slid beneath the sheet. "Just for tonight," he agreed.

Israel stared at the two in the bed. Cailyn shifted, cracked one eye, and stared at him sleepily. "You comin' to bed, or are you just gonna stand there?" She shimmied a bit and her skirt came sailing out from beneath the sheet.

Still Israel stood. Waiting.

"She needs you, man." Roman put his back to Cailyn and Israel. "Don't be too loud. I wanna get some sleep."

Israel swayed as he stared at the bed. He asked for this, not the other way around. Just for tonight he could pretend he was part of a threesome. "Fuck it." Fatigue and pain had him stripping off his clothes as he staggered toward the bed. He was completely naked when he slid beneath the sheets and next to Cailyn's warm, curvy body.

"Finally," came the pithy retort as the light clicked off.

"You've both made me so happy." She curled into Israel, tucking his arm in at her waist.

He allowed the warmth of her words to bloom through him. All he had to do was stay in the moment, his body pressed to Cailyn's and Rome a mere fingertip away.

Cailyn kissed Israel's forearm then Roman's back. "Thank you."

Israel nuzzled her neck before he closed his eyes. He never would've thought he'd be in his ex-best friend's bed with their woman. How they could make this permanent was his last thought before succumbing to sleep.

CHAPTER TEN

Gentle hands. Hot mouth. Soft moan. Cailyn arched into sensation. Hands gripped hers as she tried to squirm away from the torturous mouth between her legs.

"Too much," she gasped. Pleasure rivaled on pain. The man eating her out seemed to know how to keep her poised on the razor's edge.

Soft lips covered hers. She poured lust and heat into the kiss. Tongues dueled as the orgasm built.

They parted, gasping for air. She opened her eyes to find Israel staring down at her, a lopsided grin matching his lopsided 'fro.

She looked down her body. Roman flashed her a wicked grin before he latched onto her little pearl. She'd have come off the bed if not for Roman's hands gripping her thighs and Israel holding her hands.

"Enjoy." Israel kissed her again as she slid beneath a wave of pulsing need. The bed shifted. The hands holding her thighs released and slid away, signaling Roman leaving the bed. Israel blanketed her body. Before she could draw a breath, he was inside her. Hard. Fast. In. Out.

There was no time for thought. Just sensation. Pleasure. And then she was flying apart. Israel groaned his release and fell beside her.

Roman leaned over and kissed her. She tasted herself on his mouth.

"I gotta go to work. Otherwise I'd stay longer." He tweaked one nipple, setting off a flurry of aftershocks.

"Fuck, man." Israel breathed.

Laughing, Roman disappeared into the adjoining bathroom. A moment later the shower came on.

Cailyn lie there boneless, sweat cooling on her body. She wasn't sure if she was awake or dreaming.

"Did we hurt you?"

She shifted to bring Israel into focus. Concern and vulnerability were on full display. He reached out and righted her necklace until it hung in the hollow of her throat.

"Not at all."

Tension eased from his shoulders. He touched her cheek. "We were being gentle."

"It gets rougher?"

"It can." He grinned then sobered. "I know we still have a lot to work out, but I wanted one moment without all the drama. You were so happy and relaxed last night, and I just—" He looked away.

"Just what?" she prompted.

"Wanted to see that look on your face again. I know I'll probably do some self-sabotage shit later, but for now I wanted…" He tugged at his afro. "I dunno. Maybe I needed the moment too."

"There's nothing wrong with needing something. Or someone."

He leaned over and kissed her. "I don't want to fuck this up. You mean so much to me. And the way things went down with Nika…"

She placed a finger against his lips. "I'm not her." She let the words hang there. "I will never be her. We've been together long enough for you to know I will not intentionally hurt you. Even when you give in to your temper."

He managed a self-deprecating smile.

"Thank you for wanting to see me happy. And when we get everything all talked out, I'd like to see what the two of you do when you're not holding back."

As if in answer, his erection bobbed against her thigh. "At least one head knows what it wants."

She scrunched his 'fro. "Eventually the two will line up."

The bathroom door opened and Roman appeared with a towel low on his hips. "Shower's free." He crossed to the dresser, pulling out underwear and a t-shirt.

Cailyn scooted to the edge of the bed, allowing the sheet to puddle to the floor. "That's my cue. I've got a few meetings at work."

Israel started to follow. "I thought you were staying here."

"I can't. If I disappear, then whoever is behind this will know I know," she said.

"Cailyn, I really think it would be better if you stay here," Israel argued.

Roman slipped into the boxer briefs then pulled the t-shirt over his head. He padded to the closet.

"Aren't you going to say something?" Israel demanded.

"Uh uh." Cailyn fisted hands on her hips. "For the record, I am not hiding out. I will be at work, in a public space with people around.

Israel stepped forward and she held up a hand. He arched a brow.

"Both of you are extremely tempting, and it's taking all my self-control not to jump you both and make us all late for work. But I do need to work." She backed into the bathroom. "And there are files I can only access at work." With that, she closed and locked the door.

"Well damn," Israel murmured.

"Our lady is pretty feisty," Roman agreed. He was now fully dressed in a pair of slacks and a simple button-down. He sat in a nearby chair to don socks and a pair of sturdy boots.

"You can't be so nonchalant about this." Israel stared at the man, incredulous.

"I'm having lunch with her later. You can drive her to work. Give her one of those fancy panic buttons."

Israel's gaze slid to the closed bathroom door. "What makes you think I have a panic button?"

Roman clapped him on the shoulder. "Because you wouldn't be you if you didn't." He walked to the bedroom door. "Thank you for last night and this morning. It means a lot to have you here and even more that we were able to share Cailyn. I've missed that."

Before Israel could say anything, Roman left.

"Well damn. We do have a lot to talk about."

Roman sat behind his desk. He was supposed to be going over his notes but couldn't keep his mind on task. Every time he read Paul's name, he thought about Cailyn and Israel in bed.

At some point during the night, the three of them were intertwined, as if they'd slept together for years. Having a morning delight before work... How he wanted to stay and do so much more. But he hadn't wanted to press the delicate truce he and Israel forged. Sleeping together and then eating her out while Israel watched and held her down? That was more than he could've hoped for. Leaving the two of them to take a shower was one of the most difficult things he'd done in a long while.

Even after the shower, the scent of sex still hung in the air, and he wanted to drag them both back to bed. But he had to work.

Perusing his notes from the shoot-out, he frowned. He'd gotten a good look at the shooter, but there still weren't any leads. He leaned back in his chair, placed his feet on the desk, and closed his eyes.

What did he know? Someone was embezzling money from Cailyn's firm. One accountant was already dead. Her office had been searched and her computer hacked. Someone was targeting her intern as well.

He pursed his lips, slowly exhaling. Something... Something was eluding him. He wasn't sure if it was something she'd said or something he'd seen. He replayed the conversations through his head. Was it something Cailyn said last night? He could almost grasp the sliver of the thought...

"Since when do you blatantly nap on the job?" a deep male voice teased.

And just like that, the thought was gone. "Lt. knows I do my best thinking in this position," Roman replied without opening his eyes. "Who let you outta your cubicle, Jenkins?"

"Must be a helluva case."

A soft thump forced his eyes open. He looked first at the thick folder on the desk then up at the newcomer.

"I brought you a little gift. Tell Rael he owes me two."

When Roman looked up again, the man was gone. A slow smile spread his lips. He opened the folder and gasped. As casually as possible, he moved the folder beneath his stack of notes then transferred the whole stack to his file bag. He would need to go over this in the privacy of his home. In the meantime, he drew his keyboard closer and typed in the URL for Cailyn's firm. Something about one of the partners dying. Once he had the man's name, Roman opened another tab and typed the name in the search engine. He'd clicked on the link with the obit when he heard his name.

"Dagon!"

Roman paused in reaching for the phone on his desk. He stared in the direction of the commanding voice. "Lt.?"

"My office. Now!"

Roman dropped his bag in the bottom drawer then locked it. He pocketed the key and stood. "What's up?" He closed the office door behind him. He paused as he caught sight of the bulky man seated in one of the leather club chairs. While the man's cheap leather shoes were well polished, the rest of him was spilling from a badly wrinkled suit. The pants were so worn they were shiny. This was in stark contrast to his lieutenant. A Black man with a caramel complexion scowled beneath a neat beard and mustache. Dark brown eyes held depth, wisdom, and knowledge of what one human being could do to another. The crisp gray dress shirt was paired with a charcoal gray and blue pinstripe tie. The suit jacket, a soot black, hung from a hanger on a coat-tree behind the desk.

"I see the rat squad is in the house." Roman sniffed. This was the same officer who had investigated the incident the last time he and Israel were partners. Roman did not like the man then or now.

"Dagon," Lt. Wallace admonished.

He held his Lt.'s gaze. "Mind telling me why we are having this little confab?"

"There are some concerns regarding the DB found in your companion's home as well as the shoot-out," Wallace began.

"And there was an altercation between you and your ex-partner," Connors, the man in the shiny suit, put in.

"The altercation was personal, and I had no idea it would happen." Roman glanced between the two. "I feel like I should have my rep in attendance."

"Roman, you're not making this easy."

"Then spit it out, Lieutenant."

"I need your shield and weapon. Until we get this resolved, you're suspended with pay."

Wordlessly, Roman placed his badge on the desk and placed his police-issued weapon next to it. Without a backward glance, he turned on his heel and left. He paused long enough to retrieve his bag from the locked drawer and make sure nothing else of importance was on his desk. Shock would come later, but for now, a cold rage simmered.

Cailyn washed her hands at the sink and stared in the mirror without seeing her reflection. She'd actually slept with both her men. The automatic faucet shut off and she waved her hand beneath the sensor so she could finish rinsing off the soap. Once done she dried her hands with the extremely loud and not quite hot enough hand dryer. What she wouldn't give for old-fashioned paper towels. Maybe if she prepared a cost-analysis for the towels vs. the electricity and upkeep spent for the dryers. Oh wait. Someone already had.

Shaking her head, she left the bathroom. She tried going about her day as normal, but every time she moved her legs, she thought about the slight ache from Roman's stubble and Israel's vigorous lovemaking. Her breath quickened. *God.* Both men.

She paused at the empty cubicle she'd commandeered for some of her work. Well, the work she hadn't wanted monitored from her desktop. She picked up several folders, hard copies of files she'd reconciled, and walked them to the department head.

"Have you noticed things are getting a little weird around here?" Jill Sands queried as she accepted the folder Cailyn handed her.

"What do you mean?"

"It seems like half the interns have disappeared, and to make matters worse, I heard that Avery was murdered."

Cailyn gasped. Was that the man in her bedroom? But why was he there? "Murdered? Are you sure?"

Jill nodded. She leaned close to Cailyn and dropped her voice to a conspiratorial level. "I also heard HR discovered evidence of embezzlement or some irregularities." This was said with an eye roll. "Mr. LaMont found evidence of several transfers to an offshore account in his wife's name."

Mr. LaMont was one of the founding partners. Cailyn had met the man on several occasions and knew him to be fastidious and persnickety. If the man said there were unexplained transfers, then it was gospel.

"Really?" Her heart skipped a beat. The pieces clicking into place. She had to get home and look through her notes again.

Jill again nodded. "It makes a body wonder what else is going on around here." She thumbed through the file. "When I went to school, my instructors drilled into us the need to be honest, scrupulous, and ethical."

"We must've have the same instructors," Cailyn agreed.

"Then you were trained right." The other woman shook her head. "I don't know what they're teaching nowadays, but it ain't been ethical." She glanced around then moved even closer to Cailyn. "I know Carter made partner, but before that, I always had to send his work back. The man tried everything to subvert the accounting system."

Cailyn chose her next words carefully. "I had the same problem when we were in the same department. I'm surprised he made it to partner."

"I think they needed the money after Johnson died."

That couldn't be right. The company was solid. If nothing else, this was another line of inquiry for her to tug. But Cailyn wanted to probe something Jill mentioned earlier. "I haven't seen a couple of the interns who were in our department, now that you mention it."

Jill bobbed her head, freeing a few tendrils of dark curly hair. "Yes. There was a nice young man who delivered some travel vouchers to me." She clicked her tongue. "Now he would make a good accountant when the time comes. Has a real sharp eye for details."

"Really?"

"Yes. I gave him some old files to go over, like I normally do, and he found a few discrepancies right off. He then asked if he could see more just to be sure he wasn't wrong or misinterpreting the data."

"And?" Cailyn prompted.

Jill shrugged. "I let him have access to the files. He came back later and said he was wrong." She paused as if lost in thought. "You know, he didn't seem so convinced about the outcome."

"Do you know which file it was?"

"Funny you should ask; it was one of Johnson's old files. Like five years back. The, uh, Lauderdale deal."

Cailyn nodded. "I'm not familiar with that one."

"That account closed just after Johnson went out for medical."

Something clicked and Cailyn made a big show of looking at her watch. "Look at the time. I've got a meeting with the Hanson Group. If I don't skedaddle, I'll be late."

"And they are all about punctuality." Jill chuckled as she walked into her office. Pausing on the threshold, Jill turned and looked at Cailyn. "You know, that intern looks a lot like Johnson. Don't you think?"

She thought she kept the surprise off her face.

"Yep. You've noticed it too. Well let me know how your meeting goes." And the door closed.

Reeling, Cailyn stood, trying to get her lungs to work and her legs to cooperate. She had to get home and think. She suppressed the urge to run to the elevator, but she did walk briskly to the call button. She jabbed the button until the doors opened. She hesitated at the sight of the lone occupant of the car.

"Well hello, Cailyn. You're just the woman I wanted to see."

"Are you sure this is where the money is going?" Israel paced the space behind TJ's chair.

He'd spent his time chasing down leads in an effort not to think about the great time he had with Cailyn. And Rome. If he examined sleeping with both of them, sharing Cailyn with Roman, Israel would find something wrong with the exchange. Already he could feel the doubts and insecurities knocking.

Had Cailyn preferred Roman's kisses to his?

Would she rather have Roman fucking her this morning instead of eating her out?

Or maybe Cailyn wanted Roman to hold her hands, hold her down?

He huffed, resisting the urge to pound his fist to his temple. Instead he continued pacing, ignoring TJ's scowls.

"I'm getting real tired of you dissing my comp skills, man. If this is where the money is going, it's where the money is going."

"So, put a hold on the money." Vibrations tickled his hip. *Finally.* He pulled out his phone.

"Is that what your boy is saying?"

Israel studied the text on his phone. He held up a finger to TJ then typed in a number.

"What does this mean?"

"Someone is accessing her work terminal." TJ tapped some keys. "Look, man, if I flag this transaction, it will eventually get back to the people you're trying to bust."

"Then do it in such a way that it looks like there's a bank error or something." Israel mumbled. The text on his phone was not making any sense.

"Your boy already told me what to do with the money. I don't need you breathing down my neck with this, Israel." TJ pounded more keys then pushed off to roll to another terminal at the end of the row. There he checked lines of code scrolling down the screen. He pushed back and resumed his place at the keyboard.

Israel's phone vibrated in his hand and he answered it. "H—"

"I need you to meet me back at my place now," Roman said without preamble.

"Well hello to you too," Israel quipped.

"I've just been suspended for our little altercation, Rael. I'm really not in the mood to play nice."

Israel swallowed hard. Another example of how his temper damaged Roman again. He strangled the guilt and pushed it deep. "They what?" He closed his eyes. "Look, man. Dammit. I didn't mean...."

A sigh burst through the line. "Just meet me at my place." The line clicked off.

"I've got to go, TJ. Keep me posted on the dollars," Israel requested.

TJ gave him a head nod and continued his work on the computer.

Cailyn slipped her hand inside her pockets as she walked into the elevator. "You've been looking for me?" she queried, hoping her apprehension did not show.

"It seems some of the files I warned you about are making themselves known."

As the doors closed, she stepped forward and stabbed the button for her floor. "That is unfortunate, as I left the files where you told me." She returned her hand to her pocket, fingering her phone as she did.

He moved closer to her and she backed away as far as the small confines of the space would allow. "You've been asking questions."

She lifted her chin in defiance. "I'm an accountant; it's my job to ask questions when the numbers don't match." She held his gaze. "Do you have something to hide, Harold?"

He glanced at the numbers above the door. "Some things are best left unsaid."

The elevator pinged and the doors slowly slid open. "Looks like this is your floor." He stepped away as if nothing had happened. "Good day, Ms. Finch."

Shaken, Cailyn hurried from the car on wobbly legs. She patted her pockets, thankful she still had her keys. She didn't need to go to her office. She bypassed her door and continued down the hall to the emergency stairs. Harold had not said anything, but his demeanor left her in a state of high alert. If Harold sliding into her personal space had the ability to unnerve her, then she needed to be someplace safe.

Bright afternoon sunlight greeted her as she escaped the office building. She didn't breathe a sigh of relief until she was locked in her vehicle. She patted her pockets, this time something thwacked against her phone. Intrigued she pulled out the contents, surprised to find a thumb drive.

Cailyn lifted her gaze, scanning the parking ramp for anyone who could be watching her. Not wasting more time, she started the car, put it in reverse, and backed out the parking space. She nosed the selector into Drive and sped from the garage.

She fumbled for the Bluetooth option on her steering wheel. Ringing filled the car as she sped toward her condo. She needed to hear one of her men's voices. With Roman at work, she figured her best bet would be Israel. She just needed to hear his voice.

"Pick up. Please pick up," she muttered, drumming her fingers on the wheel.

"Please tell me you're not in the office," Israel said.

Relief was quickly replaced with concern. "No. I'm on my way home. Why? What happened?"

She slowed for a stop sign, not quite braking all the way. Since no other vehicles were present, she rolled through. Every fiber of her being urged her toward the safety of home. Even if it was Rome's apartment. She felt safer in the confines of his walls than her office. She could take what she'd learned and tell the guys, and they would all sort it out.

"Is that Cailyn?" Rome asked in the background.

"Tell him I'm fine." She braked at a red light. "Wait. What is he doing home? His shift isn't over."

Unseeing she stared at the cross traffic. The six lanes seemed extra busy for midday. She checked the clock. There were still a couple of hours until rush hour, or rather early rush hour. Were all these people coming from lunch?

"Neither is yours," Israel pointed out.

"Something happened," she began. The light changed. She moved with the traffic, each block bringing her closer to home.

"Are you okay?"

"Just a little shaken," she admitted. "I honestly don't know what happened."

"Where are you now?"

"On MLK before it crosses Lee Street. The bridge is a bit backed up." A glint of light caught the corner of her eye a heartbeat before a large dark vehicle filled her window.

A faint screech and bang made Israel jump.

"You get shocked?" Rome teased. The smile dying on his lips as he caught sight of the horror on Israel's face.

"We need to go." Israel's voice was eerily calm. Tension and something akin to fear rolled off him in veritable waves.

The distress was so palatable, Rome reached for the weapon no longer at his side. The last time he'd seen Israel display this magnitude of emotion, he'd stared down the business end of a shotgun. There was no gun-wielding maniac now, just a phone to his former friend's ear. And a voice filled with disturbing calm, devoid of emotion. "Rael?"

Israel moved with deliberate swiftness, the phone stuck to his ear as he gathered keys. "We need to go."

Rome paused long enough to retrieve a weapon from a front closet. He checked it, grabbing two extra magazines. These he shoved in the empty holster before hurrying after Israel. Something was definitely wrong. A gnawing ache in his gut had him thinking Cailyn was in danger. Danger neither of them had foreseen.

They bypassed the elevator and ran down five flights of stairs.

"Israel?" he prompted once they burst into the early afternoon sunshine. They jogged toward Israel's SUV.

"She's been in an accident," he answered in that same toneless calm.

Rome nodded, took the keys from Israel's lax fingers, and jumped in the driver's seat. "Tell me where."

Three minutes later Israel and Rome parked on the sidewalk out of the flow of traffic, which was snarled in both directions. They jogged their way through parked cars, lookie-loos and first responders until they got to the sight of the wreckage. A pickup truck was embedded in the front driver side panel. Tiny shards of safety glass littered the road and the inside of the car. Dark liquid that bared a resemblance to blood streaked the window and headrest. The front passenger side door was open.

Rome reached for his shield, belatedly remembering he no longer had it. "Do you see her?"

Israel swiveled left and right. Fear clouded his eyes. Roman could relate, but he couldn't afford to give into the anxiety clawing in his gut. He had to stay calm, first for Cailyn. God, if he lost it now, neither he nor Israel would get through the next few minutes.

"Do you see her?" Rome repeated.

Israel shook his head. "What if she…?"

"Don't think like that," Rome admonished. He stood on tiptoe and finally spied a paramedic near the back of an open rig. "There." He pointed.

Both men made their way to the large yellow-and-white emergency vehicle. Seated on the bumper was Cailyn. She held an ice pack to her head.

"You're okay," Israel said, buckling with relief. He knelt on the ground in front of her, his legs no longer able to support him. "I heard the accident."

She reached out a trembling hand and he clasped it with his. Hot tears dropped on their joined hands. She set the ice pack aside. "Airbags save lives."

Rome swept gentle fingers over the bandage at her temple. He cleared the emotion from his throat before speaking. She was okay. A little dented and bruised but alive. "Where's the other driver?"

"Hit-and-run," the paramedic said. "When we arrived, she was the only occupant we found. She's still a little dazed." He stood then handed her a bottle of water. "You are a very lucky woman. A few more inches either way and that wouldn't have been an accident you walk away from."

"Did you see the other driver?" Rome held her gaze.

She shook her head then winced. "Can I go home now? I just want to leave."

The paramedic frowned, placing the ice pack back in her hand and guiding it to the bump on her head. "You really should go to the hospital. You've got a pretty nasty bump on your head, and there could be other injuries." He lightly touched her left arm and she winced. "And you should get this checked out."

Israel cupped her cheek with infinite tenderness. "Let them take you to the hospital, I'll be right here with you."

"I don't want to spend the next fourteen hours in emergency," she protested. She flicked her gaze between the two men.

"Rome?" Israel asked, looking for backup.

He glanced up from his phone. "She has a point."

"You're seriously going to encourage her not to get medical attention?" Israel demanded, springing to his feet. "She's in shock. And injured."

Rome patted the air in an attempt to calm the other man. "Slow your roll," he snapped. "She can't go to Urgent Care because she's been in an accident with a head injury." He tucked a curl behind her ear. "Honey, you're hurt and need to be seen by a doctor. Rael will ride with you and I'll meet the two of you at the Cape Coral Hospital near the condos. I need to check out a few things beforehand."

The two men exchanged a meaningful glance before they parted ways.

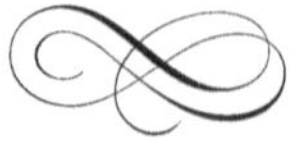

Nearly four hours later, Cailyn rested in a private hospital room with a mild concussion. Her sprained left wrist was encased in a brace. An ice pack rested over the brace so only her slightly swollen fingers peeked out. Israel sat at the head of her bed. Rome sat on the other side, his hand resting on her thigh.

"I can't believe the two of you are making me stay here overnight," she murmured. "They are not going to let me get any sleep."

"At least you didn't have to wait in the ER for a bed," Israel pointed out. "The Emergency room wasn't that busy and they got you settled fairly quick."

"But my car. And this." She lifted her hand, letting the ice pack fall to the bed. "I can't even get into my condo because it's still considered a crime scene." Tears were dangerously close. Cailyn blinked rapidly, but a few tears slid unbidden. "Why can't I just go home?"

"They just want to keep you for observation," Roman soothed. With a thumb, he brushed away a tear. "Don't cry. Everything you mentioned can be replaced or cleaned."

Cailyn drew in a stuttered breath, reeling in her errant emotions. "Right. You're right."

Now a sly smile creased his lips. "I don't mind you sharing my place until things are settled with your condo."

A faint smile creased her lips, as he intended. "I could just as easily stay with Israel."

The man in question now stood in front of the three large windows. His hands were jammed deep in his pockets. His back and shoulders tense.

"As long as I get to watch." Rome replaced the ice on her wrist.

"Thanks," she mumbled.

Roman smoothed a strand of hair from her face.

"One of us should've been with you," Israel muttered.

"What?" Cailyn couldn't be sure she'd heard him correctly.

"If Roman or I had been driving, you wouldn't have been injured."

After a glance at Roman and his subtle nod, she chose her words carefully. "No, Israel. You do not get to take the blame for this. If you or Roman had been driving, one of you could be in this bed, or worse." She reached out her good hand and he gripped her fingers. "You couldn't have known someone would run into me. It was an accident."

Now it was Israel's turn to look at Roman, who nodded.

With a sigh, Israel stared directly into Cailyn's eyes, aware he was squeezing her fingers. He loosened his hold. "The investigators said the other driver never even braked. The accident was deliberate."

She gasped. "But, oh goodness." She slumped into the pillows, allowing the implication to fully manifest. The accident hadn't been an accident. Someone tried to hurt her, or worse. She knew the statistics for hit-and-run drivers in Florida. Had someone been trying to capitalize on that as a way to kill her?

Soft lips brushed hers. "You mean so much to me, Cailyn."

She touched her forehead to Israel's. "I know. That's why I called. I knew Roman was working and wouldn't be able to answer his phone, and I couldn't wait for a text." She looked over at Roman, imploring him to understand. He flashed her a quick smile. Some of her guilt eased at the small gesture. "I needed to hear your voices. I needed you both."

"You've got us." Israel spoke up quickly.

"Let's start at the beginning. Why were you coming home early?" Roman queried.

She slowly turned to look at him. "I could ask you the same question."

"It seems we're getting really close to finding your thief and the little fight in your apartment didn't help," Roman said.

She touched his face. "I'm so sorry."

"Not your fault, baby girl. Now if Rael would apologize."
Israel glared.

Roman chuckled. "Now you."

"One of the department heads was sharing some office gossip." Cailyn quickly filled them in on what Jill had told her. "So when I got in the elevator, Harold got in my space. He really rattled me."

"Did he touch you? Threaten you?" Israel demanded.

"Not really. It was more like he was reminding me of what I shouldn't do," she said.

"What was that?" Roman said.

"He warned me about the files I'd taken to him and then said..." She closed her eyes as she recalled the words. "He said some things are better left unsaid."

"But he didn't touch you?" Roman asked again.

"No, he was just in my space." She opened her eyes. "When I got to my car, I found a flash drive in my pocket."

Israel whipped out his phone.

"Where is it?" Roman asked.

"In my skirt pockets," she admitted.

Roman went to the small closet where her clothes were stored. He rifled through the pockets a moment before he reappeared with the drive. Israel closed his phone.

"TJ is on his way," he announced.

"You think Harold slipped this in your pocket while the two of you were in the elevator?" Roman wanted to know.

"Well it wasn't there when I was talking to Jill. I tried recording the conversation on my phone, but the accident smashed the screen," Cailyn said.

"TJ can get what we need," Israel assured her.

She nodded. "I'm so glad you two are here. I've never been so scared in my life. I love you two so much."

Roman gently twined her fingers with his, while Israel held her other hand.

"I didn't mean for any of this to happen." Tears seeped from beneath her lashes. "I should've just left the whole thing alone."

"Never apologize for doing the right thing." Israel's tone was vehement. "The person to blame is the one embezzling from your company."

"And you could never have turned a blind eye to theft. That's not who you are, Cailyn. You have integrity in every aspect of your life. Personal and professional," Roman reminded her.

"The world would be a better place if there were more people like you." Israel brushed a kiss against her lips. "Rest, sweetheart. Rome and I will be here until they discharge you."

"Absolutely!" Rome agreed. "No one is going to take you from us."

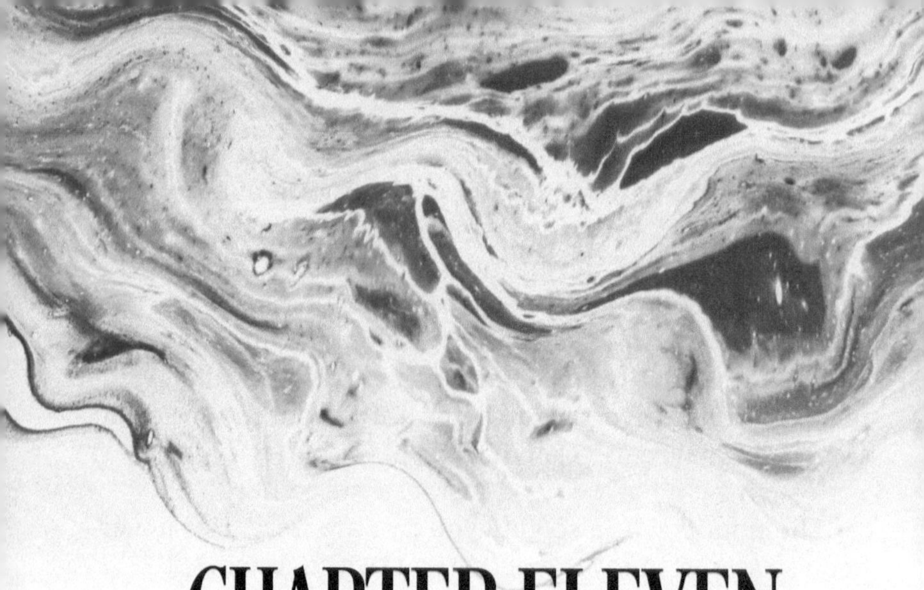

CHAPTER ELEVEN

Late the next afternoon, Cailyn sat in the middle of the couch. The first thing her men had done for her on arriving home was to help her shower off the sweat and antiseptic smell of the hospital. Next was washing and combing her hair. Now she was snug in warm pjs and Roman's thick bathrobe. The men sat on either side of her.

"Your car is totaled," Roman informed her.

She groaned. "It wasn't even two years old."

"Well now you get to shop for another one." Roman offered her a lopsided grin.

"If you tell me what you want, I'll get it for you," Israel said quietly.

She squeezed his hand. "I'll have to think about it." She turned her attention to the thick file on the coffee table. "So what's in the file?"

"Interesting you should ask. It's actually something Israel requested."

Israel widened his eyes. "Me?"

Rome nodded. "It seems the vic in your apartment and another vic had the same weapon used on them."

"Really?" Israel leaned forward and pulled the file closer. He thumbed through the thick stack of papers until he came to the autopsy reports. "Did anyone realize that these two people had a connection to the accounting firm?"

Cailyn jerked forward. "What? Who?" she demanded, trying to read over his shoulder.

Rome stroked his chin. "Now that's very interesting."

Israel held the paper just out of reach. "Be still, sweetheart, or I'll tie you to the bed and leave you there."

"You wouldn't dare."

Israel allowed her a smoldering glance before he went back to the file. "Oh I absolutely would if you weren't injured."

"I've got some hemp in the closet I've been eager to try out," Rome offered. He cast her a speculative gleam. "Perhaps when she's more herself, we can indulge in a little fantasy I've been harboring, Rael?"

The air in the room seemed to hold its breath as the two men met and held one another's gaze. The moment stretched so long, Cailyn reached a hand for each of them. Apparently the uneasy truce of a day ago was over. She lowered her head.

"I'm nothing like her," she stated, unable to keep the sadness and weariness from her voice. "The two of you know that."

"Did you know a Benjamin Cooper?" Israel asked instead.

"I... No, he doesn't ring a bell." She stood on wobbly legs. "I think I need to lie down."

Israel was on his feet a second before Roman. She waved them aside.

"I can make it to the bedroom on my own." She turned so neither man could see the sudden tears racing down her cheeks. "Israel, Roman, I love you two so much, there are days I can't believe how blessed I am to have you both in my life."

Helplessly, they watched her shuffle into the bedroom and close the door. Israel glared at Roman.

Roman settled back on the sofa with his own stack of papers. "I wonder if she has a list of employees."

"You know she went in there because of that remark about the rope."

Roman winged a brow. "No, she went in there because we need time to settle our differences."

"Dammit, Roman, you always do this!"

"Do what?" he demanded with deceptive calmness.

"Make me out to be the bad guy."

"Oh you don't need my help to do that."

Israel slammed down his sheaf of papers. "Fuck."

"She's nothing like Nika," Roman stated. "Can you honestly tell me you would've reacted like you did if Nika had been in an accident while you were on the phone? You weren't even that calm when that fool stabbed me in the neck."

Israel paused, caught off-balance by Roman's observation. No, Israel hadn't been that calm. He'd been a raving lunatic, forgetting all training, punching the suspect until he'd lost consciousness. Roman was closer than a mere friend or partner; he'd considered him his brother. And he'd lost that in one moment of inattention. But with Cailyn? All sound seemed to go out of the world. As soon as he'd heard the initial crunch and scream, the ground beneath him seemed to fall away. Cailyn was his reason for living and breathing. Being with her made his days livable and lovable again, something he hadn't had since he'd walked out of the precinct long ago.

Since he'd severed his friendship with Roman.

Did he still want to keep his friend at a distance or repair what had been broken?

"If it bothers you to do a ménage à trois with me, I won't ask for it again," Roman began. "But you know we were always better together." He glanced toward the closed bedroom door. "I enjoyed sharing her with you. She enjoyed being with both of us last night. She needed that. I needed that."

He didn't want to hear that, not when he felt the same way. But he couldn't surrender to the vulnerability, so he did what he did best. "Why can't you find your own woman?" Israel demanded. "Do you always have to have what I have?"

Roman studied him for a long moment. Disappointment and maybe resignation filled his irises. Israel couldn't bear the condemnation and looked away.

A door creaked open and a rumpled Paul padded into view. He stifled a wide yawn then eyed the two men warily. "Uh, is Cailyn all right?"

"She's a little banged up, but she's resting," Roman answered without looking from Israel. "She wanted me to reiterate that you're welcome here as long as it takes to get things worked out at the office."

Paul glanced from one man to the other. "If it's all the same to you, I'd rather visit my grandparents. They live on a farm in Pennsylvania. They're community isn't big on outsiders either, so I'll be safe."

"That sounds like a very safe place to be," Roman agreed.

Israel shuffled the papers. "Does the name Benjamin Cooper mean anything to you?"

Paul scratched a stubbled jaw and frowned. "If I'm not mistaken, he was an intern, but we weren't in the same group. As a matter of fact, we had a class or two together before he graduated. He was a year ahead of me."

"Do you know where he is now?" Israel questioned.

"He got some cushy job at an out-of-state firm. At least that's what I heard," Paul answered.

Israel opened his mouth to correct him, but Roman shook his head. "Thanks. When did you want to leave? We'll arrange for someone to travel with you until you reach your destination."

Paul grinned. "Actually tonight."

A knock sounded on the door. Israel glanced at Roman. "Expecting company?"

Roman shook his head.

Israel motioned for Paul to head back to the bedroom as he drew his pistol. Roman eyed him.

"You know how to shoot that thing?"

"Blindfolded." He grinned.

Roman removed his own weapon. "Well don't hurt yourself." He walked toward the door, staying off to the left where his shadow wouldn't cross the peephole. "What?"

"It's TJ," the voice called.

Roman glanced at Israel, who shrugged. Roman unlocked and pulled the door open in one fluid motion. TJ threw his hands up as Roman greeted him with the business end of his pistol. With one hand, he drew TJ into the foyer as he looked left and right into the empty corridor. Satisfied the hacker was alone, Roman closed the door then returned his weapon to its holster.

"Took you long enough." Israel holstered his weapon as well.

TJ placed a hand on his chest. "You two are jumpier than a whore waiting on a pregnancy test. I told you I wouldn't get here until today." He sank to the floor.

"I do have furniture," Roman said, nudging him with his foot.

"Here is good. It's not every day I stare into the barrel of two guns." He removed his bag from his shoulder. "How is your D-i-D?"

Roman winged a brow.

"Damsel in distress," Israel supplied. "And she's resting."

"Kink brothers wear her out?" TJ jested.

"Car accident, TJ," Israel snapped.

TJ shrugged with a smirk. "Now where is this flash drive?"

Israel disappeared into the bedroom while Roman crouched next to TJ. "Any movement on the money?"

TJ shook his head. "Nope. Got it bogged down in the world wide web."

"How long can you keep doing that?"

TJ grinned in response.

Israel returned but diverted to the other bedroom to give the all clear. He tossed the drive in Roman's direction. He plucked it from the air with ease.

TJ opened his laptop then inserted the drive into a USB port. After a few minutes, he let out a low whistle. "Very neat. The entire operation is laid out for the world to see." He turned the computer so the other men could view the info.

"Yes, but who's behind the embezzlement?" Roman mused.

"When the money don't hit the account, they'll start looking for your D-i-D, so be warned." TJ tapped some keys, ejected the drive, then handed it back to Roman. "Welp, my work here is done. I'll keep you posted on the money, and if I get any more information, I'll let you know that too." He stuffed his laptop back in its bag then stood. "Deuces."

Roman looked at Israel. "How long do you think we have before they come after her?"

Israel held his gaze. "We will keep her safe."

Harold sat at his desk. He kept one eye on the clock while he typed frantically on his keyboard. Once Carter found out what he'd done, his life would be over. He had to get whatever he could and get out of the country, or at least put several states between them.

He clicked, dragged, then typed more keys. A sigh of relief brushed past his lips as the little mail icon switched to sending. The door banged against the wall. Harold jumped back as Carter stormed into the room.

"Where is my money?" he demanded.

Harold shook his head. "You are getting paranoid. Your money is right where you left it." He shifted his gaze back to his computer in the hopes the other man wouldn't see his hands trembling.

"If it was where I left it, I wouldn't be here now, would I?" The silky purr did little to hide the menace in his voice.

"I did what you asked me to. Contrary to popular opinion, I do not control the internet."

Crack! Pain exploded in Harold's head, and for a moment, he wondered how the stars could be so bright while he was indoors.

"Don't get flippant with me! The only reason I don't shoot you now is because I need you to find my money!"

Harold blinked several times to clear his vision and then touched the tip of his tongue to the inside corner of his mouth. The salty, coppery taste of blood coated his tongue.

He reached for a tissue and dabbed at the blood.

"Feel better?" Harold asked.

"Find my money!"

Harold clicked some keys. "The transfer is still out there. You just have to wait for it to post to your account."

"It's never taken this long before."

"It's never been this large before."

"My secretary said she saw you in the elevator with that Finch woman."

Harold had to play this cool. "And did she also tell you I sent that Finch woman running scared?"

The other man's shoulder's slumped slightly. "As a matter of fact, I went looking for that meddlesome female, and she wasn't in the office. If we can't figure out who's doing this, we'll both be brought up on charges. I can't afford another scandal."

Harold tapped some keys. "Calm down. I initiated the transfer like you asked, like we always do." He trailed off. "This isn't the right account."

Stanley practically pushed Harold aside to see the computer. "What?"

Harold muscled his way back in front of the computer. "This deposit has been intercepted." He stared at Stanley. "I didn't do this."

Cailyn gingerly stretched her body, assessing the soreness of her muscles. Her entire body ached and rivaled her head for pain. Slowly she sat up, wary. Something had disturbed her sleep and she wasn't sure if it had been voices or something else. Stifling a grown, she swung her legs out of bed and stood. She swayed a bit, waiting for the nausea to settle and the room to right itself. Once it had, she shuffled across the floor to the door, pressing her ear to the cool wood. Voices, but they were tense. She slowly turned the knob and eased the door just far enough to press her eye to the gap. Israel pointed a gun at the front door. From her vantage point, she couldn't see Roman. Apprehension tightened her stomach and she forgot all about the pain in her body.

She held her breath, unable to look away. The front door crashed open. Shoes squeaked on the wood, clothing rustled, and the skinny frame of TJ appeared in her vision before he slumped against the wall.

Israel shook his head then reholstered his weapon. "Seriously?"

Cailyn sagged against the door in relief. Sudden tears burned her eyes. She must've made a sound because Israel turned her way. She moved away from the door, but Israel pushed through the opening a moment later.

"This is all my fault," she wept.

Here she was, bringing trouble to someone else's home, and they were taking it all in stride. Logically, she knew this wasn't her fault, but so much had happened and she was just worn out. Crying was her only release.

Israel gathered her close. "No, sweetheart, it isn't," he soothed. "It's whoever is embezzling from your company."

"A dead guy was placed in my condo, my car is totaled, and now you and Roman are holding guns on visitors." She balled her fists in his shirt. "And Roman is suspended. Tell me that's not my fault."

Israel scooped her up and sat on the bed with her on his lap. "C'mon, sweetheart, you're killing me with your tears. Roman will be fine. You can get a new car and a new place if you want, or you can move in with me or Roman, or we can all get a place together." He'd promise her anything to get her to stop crying. "None of this is your fault." He brushed a kiss against her hair. "Roman getting suspended is my fault. I lost my temper. Not you."

Roman stood in the doorway. "TJ's gone and Paul is packing his stuff."

"Paul? Where's he going?" Cailyn said between sobs. "And the two of you are looking at me like I'm some hysterical female."

Roman offered a lopsided grin. "Well, baby girl, you are a bit emotional."

"I'm sorry you got suspended," she said.

"If they don't reinstate me, I'll buy into Israel's firm," Roman remarked lightly.

Israel stared at him.

"I just wanted to do the right thing," she murmured.

"And you are." Roman knelt in front of the couple. "You've done nothing wrong, Cailyn, so get that outta your head right now. Israel and I have chosen to stand with you through this, and no matter how hard it gets, that will never change."

"Whatever it takes," Israel agreed.

"I can't live in my place," she reminded them.

"Then you can move in with one of us, or we all find a place together," Roman offered.

She giggled through a fresh wave of tears. "Israel said the same thing."

Roman cleared her tears with his fingertips. "Your tears are our kryptonite. We will do whatever it takes to get you to stop."

"Damn straight." Israel twined her fingers with his.

Roman placed a hand over both of theirs, and Israel gave him the faintest of nods. This was their woman, and they would do whatever it took to keep her happy and safe.

He tapped the app that would give him access to the biggest deposit he'd ever received. With this money he could finally disappear, and no one would know he was the one behind the embezzlement. Everything he'd set in place led to the higher ups. He frowned. The money wasn't there.

He logged out then checked his email for any updates. He breathed a sigh of relief. Okay, just a slight delay. That was fine. He could wait another day or two, but after that, he would have to disappear. Cailyn and her friends were getting too close to him. He had to be very careful. His only consolation was that no one suspected him since he'd been the target of a shooting.

Paul smiled. That had been a stroke of genius. Just pay his buddy to fire a couple of shots, and voilà, instant innocence. Somehow he'd had to slip past the two men and not have them give him an escort to the airport. Or he could just pretend. A slow smile spread his lips. Yes, he could pretend.

CHAPTER TWELVE

Three days later Cailyn sat on the balcony, enjoying the warm summer breeze. Her accident seemed like a lifetime ago. The only reminders were the dull ache in her head and the throbbing in her wrists. She pored over a spreadsheet, tracking columns of numbers as each credit did little to balance with the debits. She closed her eyes and blew out a breath.

"You're supposed to be resting," Roman admonished as he stepped onto the balcony.

She cracked one lid to look at him. "This doesn't make sense."

He placed a plate with a salad on the table away from her papers. "Well we know that."

She shook her head. "No, all the accounts I've looked at have pointed to the partner's personal accounts." She pointed to an amount she'd underlined twice in red. "See this?"

He moved so he was now standing behind her. "Yeah."

"This amount corresponds with this one here." She indicated another account on a separate page. "Both of these are expense accounts supposedly assigned to the execs, but this number here," she tapped a string of letters and numbers in the first column, "don't correspond with any one person." She glanced at the blank look on his face. "When you do a sting and have to buy something, you get a receipt or something that says you paid for the item or logged it out."

"Right. Name, badge number, chain of custody."

"Right. Well each of these," she indicated the first column again, "pertains to everyone in the firm who has an expense account. Or any employee who turned in a receipt for reimbursement." She shuffled some papers. "Now CSP1928 appears as far back as five years, and everything is normal."

He studied the flow of numbers. "Okay, I'm with you."

"Now look at CSP1927."

"Is this the same person?"

"At first glance one would think so, but take a look at this." She handed him another page. "If you look, you can also see the corresponding voucher numbers." She shifted more papers and then thumbed through a stack of files. "I would've dismissed this myself, except I'm the one who issued these vouchers."

Roman studied the spreadsheet then the vouchers. "So who altered the vouchers?"

She shrugged. "I have an idea, but I'm not sure."

"We both heard that argument in the office, and you have the flash drive."

"What if they were arguing about something else?" she mused. "Maybe they were trying to find out the same things we are?"

"Then why wouldn't they want you to bring embezzlement to their attention?" Roman countered.

"Because it makes the firm look weak," she said. "All the protocols put in place to prevent something like this from happening failed."

"Are you sure the company wasn't hacked?"

She shook her head. "I checked. IT told me they keep the software and firewalls updated. And they have their own little hackers to keep others out. She and TJ would get along very well."

"You can introduce the two when this is over," Roman murmured as he perused the pages. "Does this tell you who worked on the accounts?"

"No. Hey, I forgot to ask if TJ could access employment records."

"Why?" He was genuinely curious now.

"Jill said something to me the day of my accident, and it just came back to me."

He pulled out his phone. "Anyone in particular?"

"The partner Johnson. Can he get the names of his children?"

He typed, his thumbs a blur. "He'll get back to us." He shuffled the papers. "Anything else?"

"Have him look into Carter Stanley."

"Isn't he one of the partners?"

"Yes."

Roman typed. "So what put him on your radar?"

"He likes to cut corners. He keeps things just shy of illegal."

"TJ will get back to us as soon as he has something."

"Thanks."

The doorbell peeled through the open door. Roman set the papers on the table. "That's probably Israel. I'll be right back."

Cailyn nodded as she returned her attention to the list of people who had worked on the accounts. She was one of them, but IT had provided her with a list of user IDs and names. Low voices provided the background noise. A bird squawked and she thought she heard a soft expletive. She paused in her movements, waiting for the noise to repeat itself. When it didn't, she resumed working.

It wasn't until something cold and hard hit the back of her head that she knew something was very wrong.

"Stand up very, very slowly, then turn around." The voice, though familiar, held none of the fear or humility she was used to hearing.

She did as ordered. "You."

Israel leaned against the door jamb of Red's office. He watched the big man work, his fat fingers flying nimbly across the keyboard.

"Please tell me you've got something?" Israel asked.

"You were always the impatient one. Why are you not taking care of your woman?" Red demanded.

"Because I need to follow up on this lead, and since you know my comp skills suck, I came to you."

"Aren't we the lucky ones," he quipped.

"I got it!" TJ yelled from behind him.

Israel whirled and hurried to the other man. "You found it?"

"Hell yeah!" TJ typed some keys and the information appeared on an upper monitor. "He tried to access the account today, and I got him." He frowned at the information scrolling on the screen. "That can't be right. The cell towers ping him as being at Roman's..."

Israel snatched out his phone on the run. He had to get to Cailyn.

The door was open when he arrived. Israel entered, gun drawn. Heart pounding, he cleared the condo room by room. At the splotch of blood on the floor, he paused. He bent and touched the droplets. Still wet. That meant whoever the blood belonged to was still here.

He followed the drops to the kitchen and met Roman's angry glare.

He snatched the dish towel from the man's mouth. "What happened?"

"He jumped me when my back was turned." Roman turned so Israel could get at the cuffs on his wrists. "He took Cailyn."

"How the hell did you let that little punk get the drop on you?" Israel holstered his weapon and then fished his keys from his pocket. He shook them out until he found the handcuff key. "He played us all. Did he truss you up like this?"

Roman shook his head and then groaned. "He forced Cailyn to do it." He held up a paring knife. "She managed to slip this to me."

"Didn't do you much good." He went to the freezer and placed several cubes of ice in the towel. He handed it to Roman. "Where'd he take her?"

"Didn't say." Roman set the towel down then cut the twine at his ankles. "How did you know it was him?"

"TJ got a ping from the cell towers just before he cut through the layers on the bank account." He studied Roman, who still sat on the floor. "Are you sure you're okay?"

"I let him in my house. We protected him, but most of all, I'm pissed I let him in my house."

Israel held out his hand. When Roman grasped it, Israel pulled him to his feet. He met and held the other man's gaze. "When we find this asshole, we put him down like a rabid dog. He hurt Cailyn."

"If I do this, there's no going back for me," Roman admitted.

Israel flashed a lopsided grin. "I've an opening for a partner."

"Then let's go get our love."

Cailyn plastered herself against the passenger door as far from her abductor as she could. "Thank you for not killing my friend."

"I like you, Ms. Finch. Things were not supposed to go down like this, but I have no choice. You weren't supposed to go outside the firm with the accounts I gave you. You were just supposed to give them to the partners and leave it alone."

She shook her head. "Why?"

He glanced at her. "Why does anybody steal? For the money." He chuckled. "It was surprisingly easy once I got my foot in the door. Jill just gave me accounts and I did what I do best."

"You're a brilliant accountant."

"Who wants to balance other people's money when it can be stolen?" he sneered. "The checks and balances were a joke. They should be thanking me for showing them how vulnerable they are."

"I don't understand any of this."

"It's very simple. Your men are going to make sure I get my money. Once I have my money, you can go."

Cailyn gripped her seatbelt as her mind raced. Yes, she could see how Paul had gotten away with embezzling so far, but there were still a few things that didn't add up. "Did you kill Spencer Avery?"

He paled. "That was an accident."

"But why in my apartment?"

"We were there to get your computer and any files you may have had."

"But someone shot at you."

"It's amazing what you can accomplish when you have a little money."

She caught movement from the corner of her eye. "Watch out!"

For the second time that week, a car plowed into the driver's side. Tires screeched and the car spun twice before coming to a hissing rest. Dazed, Cailyn looked around, but a haze blurred her vision.

With effort, she looked at Paul. He slumped in the seat, his chin resting on his chest. Moaning, he shifted, and she could now see a trickle of blood on his face. The airbag was quickly deflating. Now was the time to get away from him.

She unfastened her seatbelt and fumbled for the door. Before she could find the handle, it was wrenched open with a scream of metal on metal. Instinctively she shrank back.

She looked up to find a ski-mask-wearing man glaring at her. He gripped her arm then dragged her from the car.

Not again. She punched and scratched at the man. Her fist collided with something soft and he grunted. He released her and she fell to the hard asphalt.

"Hey!" someone yelled. "What are you doing?"

"Help!" Cailyn screamed as she scrambled away. Heat seared her hands and knees.

The man grabbed her ankle. She kicked out. Another connection.

A shot rang out. People screamed. Metal crunched on metal. Horns blared.

Cailyn finally gained her feet and took off in a stuttered run. She didn't get far before footsteps pounded behind her. A moment later something hard hit her. She collided with the unyielding ground and slid a few inches.

"You stupid, meddlesome bitch!" he hissed.

Every cell in her body screamed at her to move, to fight back, but she couldn't. The tackle knocked the wind from her, and it was all she could do to gasp in air. When he yanked her to her feet, her struggles were feeble.

He half-dragged, half-carried her toward a waiting van.

"Don't you dare double-cross me." Paul staggered from the driver's side. He waved his own weapon.

Three shots rang out. Cailyn stared in horror, uncomprehending, as bright blood bloomed on Paul's chest. Apparently he had trouble comprehending it as well. He looked down, touched the spot, then stared at his fingers. He seemed to stand suspended before locking gazes with Cailyn. His lips moved.

As if in slow motion, he crumpled to the ground. Only then did she start screaming.

Dimly she was aware of the man dragging her away. Still she couldn't get her limbs to cooperate or stop screaming. She knew she should fight, but it was as if her mind had shut down. She'd just seen someone she knew murdered before her eyes.

A sharp stinging slap to her cheek snapped her head to the side and cut off her screams. Holding her hands to her face, Cailyn stared into flat, cold eyes. Everything she needed to know about her future was in those cold, cold depths.

"Very good." He pressed the still warm barrel to the center of her forehead.

She went still. Her heart sped while her insides and joints went liquid. If the man hadn't held her so tight, she'd have puddled right there on the road. If he pulled the trigger, there would be no more nights with Israel or Roman. There wouldn't be a chance for them to work out a threesome or anything else. A slow tear whispered from her eye. She wouldn't give this man the satisfaction of her giving in.

"You can experience the same thing," he warned.

Right. If he was going through all this trouble, he needed something from her. She didn't think she had it, but the goal was to survive. Help was coming. All she had to do was stay alive long enough for her men to find her.

If they found her.

Heat and humidity did little to permeate the chill invading her body. This could be her last day on Earth and she couldn't get warm enough.

She couldn't think like that and she quashed the niggle of doubt. Forcing panic aside, she licked dry lips. "What do you want?"

"You're gonna get me the money Paul promised me." The voice was low and gravelly. "And if all goes well, you just might live."

He steered her toward a waiting van. He shoved her in the back, where he quickly tied her wrists and ankles. He then pulled out a black hood. She moved her head away.

"I could very easily kill you now and still get my money. The choice is yours."

She stared at him, chin lifted in defiance. "You intend to kill me anyway."

He chuckled. "Paul said you were smart." His eyes hardened. "Put the hood on and you live a little longer."

Cailyn closed her eyes as the hood was lowered over her head. Hot tears streamed down her cheeks and soaked the cloth. There was no way Roman and Israel could find her. The door slammed, and a moment later, the driver's door opened and closed. The seat behind her creaked as the man adjusted.

"Comfy?" He laughed. The vehicle started with a roar. Cailyn lurched forward as the van took off. She had to think. If she could stay mindful of the turns and such, maybe she could tell Israel and Rome where she was.

The hood was hot and smelled of sour milk. She rubbed her head against the seat in an effort to shift it to where she could glimpse anything. Light filtered through a small tear in the fabric. It wasn't much, but she could just make out the rear of the van.

The vehicle bumped over a large groove in the road and she tumbled sideways. Without a way to brace herself over the rough terrain, she banged her head on the metal side panel and saw stars. Nausea rolled in her belly and she fought down the bile in her throat. If she puked now, it would stay with her until her abductor decided to remove the hood. There was no way she could handle that. Slow, steady breaths were her saving grace. Once her stomach was under control, she realized the move had shifted the hood enough to where she could see an inch-wide gap, and that was just enough to allow visibility out the rear window.

They passed a McDonald's, a Burger King, a Circle K, and a Wawa before the van turned and bumped over deep pits and gravel.

She gasped and gritted her teeth against the ups and downs. In vain she did her best to brace her bound feet against the other wall. Still the uneven movement was brutal, aggravating old and new pains until her body was one large cacophony of agony. She was near tears by the time the vehicle ground to a halt. She lay on the floor, staring at a lopsided sign with faded red letters.

The front door slammed, shaking the vehicle. A moment later the side door opened and a cool breeze swept through the opening. She did not move. She didn't think she could. Her head hurt, her body throbbed, and nausea had returned with a vengeance.

"Did you not find the ride to your liking?" her captor taunted.

"Please take off the hood. I need to throw up." Even talking allowed her stomach to lurch and roll. She gagged and then retched.

Swearing, the man grabbed her under her arms and dragged her out of the van. He ripped the hood off as the first spasms of vomit projected from her mouth. The sick splattered on his shoes. "Fuck." He dropped her then proceeded to wipe his shoes in the dirt and grass.

Cailyn rolled to her side as her stomach continued to expel its contents. Her head throbbed with every spasm, and she didn't realize she was crying until several tears trailed into her ear. Blackness tapped at the sides of her vision. She lay there, panting and gasping, praying that at least that part was over.

"You filthy bitch! Look what you did to my new boots," the man raged above her.

Cailyn rolled to her other side then curled into the fetal position as much as her bonds would allow. She expected him to kick her at any moment. He seemed like that type of guy. She squeezed her eyes closed. Waiting for the angry blows.

Waiting.

Waiting.

Footsteps vibrated through the soil and she braced for impact. No more. She couldn't take any more trauma to her body.

When he nudged her, she whimpered. The sound escaping before she could stop it. Instead of a hard kick, she was jerked up and tossed over the man's shoulder. The position only made her head swim and reminded her of how raw the rest of her was.

A grunt punctuated each step. The jostling did very little to tame her addled system. Her abused stomach dug into his shoulder, and she wanted to throw up again, but there was nothing left. After about ten or twelve steps, he halted.

Where the heck were they? Sweat beaded on her face and ran into her hair. She twisted, trying to take in as much of her surroundings as possible. Nothing but green, brown, and gravel. Maybe a few dilapidated buildings. She strained to hear traffic noises but only caught bird song, insects, and the distant hum of—she cocked her head to the side—a generator? Maybe.

Metal screeched and they were moving again. The sun no longer beat down on them, but it was still hot. His footsteps echoed. So they were in a large open space. They stopped.

He dropped her unceremoniously onto a rough surface.

She landed with a thud and barely managed a yelp. He grabbed a handful of her hair and snatched her to a sitting position.

"I'd kill you right now." He shoved his face into hers. Hot spittle landed on her cheek while his fetid breath threatened to have her vomit again.

Surprise left her speechless. "You," she managed to gasp.

Carter Stanley stared at the television in horror. This couldn't be happening. He read the crawl on the bottom of the screen. One dead after car crash. He turned the volume up on the TV while he rushed around the room, throwing papers and pens off his desk in a frantic effort to find the account information.

"...as close as we can get, law enforcement are treating this as an active shooter scenario. Witnesses we've been able to interview state they stopped to help the occupants of the white vehicle when a masked man yanked the female passenger from the vehicle. When they tried to help, the assailant opened fire."

Carter tuned this out as he found the slip of paper, dropped into his leather executive chair, and pounded out the login information.

He shouldn't have trusted Harold. And he should've done something about that nosy intern Paul. There was too much money at stake for him to be so careless and arrogant. God, if he'd been tempted with all those zeroes, why not his minions?

The screen popped up and he could only stare. The money was not there.

"What are we doing here?" Israel demanded as they rode the elevator to the fifth floor.

"Cailyn asked me to have one of the partners investigated. She mentioned how he liked to cut corners."

"You think he's involved?"

The car slowed and bounced before it came to a complete halt as the doors slid open.

"I won't know until I ask him." Roman glanced at the names on the doors. Israel trailed him.

"Man, we need to have a plan. You can't go up in there half-cocked. You know this is a white dude."

"Good thing I'm equal opportunity whup ass." Roman paused in front of the last door in the corridor. He raised his hand to knock and noticed the dark space between the door and jamb. Using the back of his hand, he nudged the door open.

Papers and pens littered the floor. A chair was overturned and the executive chair was shoved against the wall behind the desk.

"This don't look good," Israel said.

Wordlessly Roman crossed the room, skirting the paper on the floor to stand behind the desk. Pulling a pen from his pocket, he used it to nudged the mouse. The screen came alive, showing a bank login screen.

"We must have just missed him." Israel crouched over one of the papers on the floor. "This looks like memos, and maybe he left in a hurry."

"Oh he's definitely involved." Roman took a picture with his phone. "This is one of the accounts Cailyn had on her list."

Israel straightened. "Well, we're not going to find anything else…"

"As we said earlier, police are still treating this scene as an active shooter."

Both men turned to stare at the television. The image showed several car accidents, along with yellow numbered crime scene markers. They didn't wait to hear more.

"Get TJ on the line," Israel ordered as they bypassed the elevator for the stairs.

"He's not picking up," Roman said as they flew down the steps two and three at a time.

"Keep trying until he picks up."

They burst into the parking garage as the phone was answered on the fifth ring.

"I can't work with all these interruptions," TJ snapped. "I said I'd call when I had something."

"The last name I sent you." Roman yanked open the passenger door as soon as Israel hit the locks. "Carter Stanley. He's involved."

Israel gunned the engine and roared out of the garage. "Wait a tick."

"We ain't got time for this!" Roman snarled.

Israel winged a brow. Was Roman losing his cool? By the silence on the phone, apparently TJ thought the same.

"I thought you were the calm one," TJ finally said.

"TJ. Give me what I'm asking or we're going to have a misunderstanding," Roman ordered.

Israel grinned as he braked for a light. "I thought I was the hothead."

"Don't start, Rael," Roman warned.

"Y'all I'm working as fast as I can," TJ said.

"Work faster," Roman growled.

"What about this shooting? I've got Stanley's cell in proximity to the shooting," TJ told them.

The two men exchanged glances. "Where?"

Keys typing filtered through the speaker. "Edison and Evans Ave."

"Have you gotten a lock on Paul's phone?" Israel demanded.

"I'm a hacker not a miracle worker."

"C'mon, TJ, work your magic and tell us the last location of Paul's phone," Roman cajoled. "I know you've hacked into the network more than once."

"Keep your boxers on straight, this ain't like flipping a switch," TJ snapped.

The handheld police scanner Israel kept clipped to the dashboard sparked to life. "Attention all units. Suspect vehicle sighted on 75 going South, past mile marker 136."

"Lats pinged at Edison and Evans," TJ said. "And it's still active."

"Thanks, TJ," Roman said. "I owe you."

"You do." With that he disconnected the call.

"Edison or follow the vehicle?" Israel asked.

"Crime scene first."

Israel stomped the gas and the car leapt forward.

"She's fine, Israel," Roman said, more for his benefit than his friend's.

"She better be or TJ will be bailing us out," Israel muttered.

Roman allowed a smile to curve his lips. He clutched his seatbelt as Israel swerved around a dump truck with barely paint to spare. Several horns blared in protest. "Chill. We won't do her any good if we're part of the pavement."

"You never complained about my driving skills before," Israel snapped.

"We weren't civilians before."

Israel bared his teeth in a grin. "Yeah, a siren does make things easier." He downshifted, changed lanes, then took a corner with a squeal of tires. He slammed on his brakes as the first of flashing lights came into view. He quickly parked the car at an angle. He and Roman exited at the same time.

Merciless heat beat on them from a cloudless blue sky while there was enough moisture in the air to drink.

By the time they jogged toward the line of emergency vehicles, both men were drenched in sweat. An ambulance was on the scene, but paramedics stood at the driver's side window. One shook his head, while an officer waved to his partner.

Roman studied the scene. Watching the scene unfold on a television screen gave the illusion of make-believe. This—a few shards of safety glass, some unidentifiable liquid, an abandoned flip-flop, a sock, and even someone crying for their mama—made it all too real. What the hell happened here?

Two other vehicles were smashed together. Another grouping of cars and trucks were haphazardly parked along and up on the curb.

"I don't see her." Israel couldn't keep the fear from his voice.

This wasn't like the last time when they found her seated in the back of an ambulance. He hoped he would see her sitting in the back of a rig. But every fiber of his being knew they wouldn't be that lucky this go-round.

Roman swallowed his own fear. There should be more EMTs. At the very least, more urgency to help the injured.

Again he scanned the area, paying close attention to the vehicles locked like some perverted T. The old truck was vacant, as was the other. Most of the attention was centered around a small group of people and a blue tent. He spied several spent shells on the asphalt. The dread he'd kept at bay shoved in and made itself known. Who was behind the blue screen?

"She's not here." Roman sighed. *Please let me be right.*

Israel turned and grabbed a fistful of his friend's shirt. "Are you sure?"

Roman stared into the other man's eyes. Fear to rival his own reflected back at him. He gently pried Israel's fingers from his shirt. "She's not here."

Roman's phone vibrated on his hip. He snatched it up. "Speak."

"He wants the money."

The background faded away. There was no radio squawks, no engine noises, or even the heat of the sun. There was only the sweet voice on the other end of his phone. He smacked Israel in the chest.

Israel frowned opened his mouth to speak.

Roman locked gazes with Israel and pointed at the phone. Israel nodded and Roman turned up the volume on the phone so they both could hear.

"Where are you, sweetheart?"

"I—" The sound of flesh on flesh followed by the cry of pain reverberated through the phone.

The men exchanged meaningful looks. Whoever had struck Cailyn would pay.

When she came back to the phone, her voice wobbled badly. "He wants the money sent to his account as it was sent before."

A faint trill split the air. Israel fumbled with his phone. He walked a few paces away. "TJ, tell me something."

"If you can keep them talking a few more minutes, I can get an exact location."

Israel turned, cradling the phone between his shoulder and ear. He placed his palms together then slowly pulled them apart, a silent message for the other man to draw the conversation on as long as possible.

Roman nodded his understanding. "Are you hurt?"

"Paul set this up. I'm so sorry I brought him to you."

Tears burned. Of all the things she thought to apologize for, she was apologizing for bringing Paul to his doorstep. Roman wiped a hand down his face. He wasn't sure if all the moisture was sweat. "Don't worry about that now, sweetheart."

"He killed Paul. Right in front of me." Her voice broke. "And he's going to kill me too."

Roman froze at the fear and absolute certainty in her voice. "Cailyn, we'll get him the money. Do whatever you have to do to survive."

"I've seen his face. He's not going to let me live."

He swallowed the lump clogging his throat. "Baby girl, we'll get him the money, and we'll get you too."

Israel flashed Roman a thumbs up and jogged toward their vehicle. Roman followed.

"Tell him we're going to get him his money, but he won't get a fucking dime if he puts his hands on you again." He disconnected the call. "Where is she?"

They jumped in the car. Israel had the vehicle on and burning rubber before Roman slammed his door closed.

"About twenty minutes outside of town. Far enough that no one will hear her scream." Israel wove in and out of traffic and cleared every yellow light with a trail of horns and middle fingers.

Roman picked up his phone and dialed TJ. "Hey, I need you to release that money."

Israel glanced at him. "What da fuck, man?"

"Watch the road!"

Israel jerked the wheel in time to avoid a collision with the rear bumper of a Mustang. He swerved into the incoming lane and slid in front of the Mustang, avoiding a head-on collision.

"Fuck!" Roman swore.

"Then don't distract me!"

"Uh, y'all good?" TJ ventured.

"I need you to make it seem like the transfer went through. Just long enough for us to get Cailyn back," Roman told him.

"You tell me when and where and I'll make his bank account sing and cry," TJ promised.

They fell silent as the road whipped by. Storefronts and apartment buildings gave way to open fields and long wooden fences. Israel slowed as they crunched over gravel-filled ruts.

He pulled over in a small copse of trees and shut off the engine. He faced Roman.

"What's the plan?"

"Whether he gets his money or not, he's going to kill her," Roman said.

"We're putting this mutha fucka down, I'm asking you how you want to play this."

"Down and dirty. He put his hands on her."

Israel nodded and shoved out the car. He popped the trunk. "Down and dirty it is."

CHAPTER THIRTEEN

Cailyn watched her former coworker pace and glance at his phone. She shivered against the rough wall and cold cement. "Why?"

"Because they cut me out of the partnership and opted for that fool Stanley. Just because he brought in more clients. It didn't matter that Stanley's practices skated this side of legal. The partners were only interested in the bottom line. It didn't matter to them that I'd been there since the beginning. That I was Johnson's assistant. LaMont allowed Stanley the spot that was rightfully mine."

"But you handed me—" She stopped. "You wanted it to look like Stanley did it."

"That's the thing, Stanley really did embezzle money."

Stunned, Cailyn gaped. "But—" She forced her mind to work. "I know your work, Harold. Stanley has always been less than ethical. What did he have on you?"

Now Harold frowned, sadness weighing down his shoulders. "You're too smart for your own good. I knew if you got your hands on Avery's accounts, you'd find the discrepancies."

She had to keep him talking. The longer he explained, the more time her men had to find her. "What happened?"

"It was stupid. Our A/C and well went out after the last hurricane. We didn't have insurance, and we'd used our savings to repair the damage to our house. We found out our youngest has an aggressive form of cancer, and we just needed to cover her medications until the health insurance kicked in." He turned sorrowful eyes to her. "I paid the money back. No one knew, but Stanley found out."

"And extorted you into helping him."

He nodded.

"You could've reported him. No one would've batted an eye."

He didn't respond or look at her.

"Because you did it again," she surmised.

"Yes."

"Did you have to kill Paul?" She blinked back fresh tears. She would never get the image of Paul falling. "You used him to get the money. It had nothing to do with who his father was."

His grin widened. "I see you figured it out. Paul got greedy and sloppy." Harold paused long enough to check his phone for messages. "I liked you, Cailyn. I really did. You're what all accountants should be. It's what I started out as. Until I let life take over."

She held his gaze. "But you're still going to kill me."

"I really have no choice. You know too much." He stopped directly in front of her. "I promise you won't suffer."

Something that sounded like tires crunching on gravel drifted through the space. Was that real or imagined? Harold flinched, turning his head as if listening. Hope flared. Maybe it was a real sound.

"Just let me go. You'll have your money, and you'll disappear to a non-extradition country. Two people are dead already; I don't have to be the third." She had to stall, give her men as much time as possible. Would they find her in time? Or would it be lights out when Harold got the money?

"Stop talking," he ordered.

She opened her mouth to protest but closed it. She heard it now too. Footsteps.

She listened. Not stealthy, but strident. Angry.

"Harold!" a male voice bellowed.

Cailyn stilled. A fresh wave of fear flowed over her. She recognized the voice.

"Dammit," Harold swore. He stalked toward the door just as Carter Stanley appeared in the opening.

"You bastard!"

"Pot. Kettle," Harold snapped.

"I want my money."

"It's my money! I did the work to get it out of the firm," Harold claimed.

"Whatever."

Harold glanced at his phone.

Stanley stepped farther into the room. "Your handiwork is all over the news."

"A little distraction while I get my money."

Cailyn scooted for the shadows. This was bad. One attacker, she could outmaneuver, but not two.

Stanley stopped, stared, then laughed. "You don't have the money."

"That's why she's here." Harold waved a hand toward the wall.

Carter turned. "Oh."

Hatred and calculation gleamed in the man's eyes. Cailyn shrank back.

"So you're the reason I don't have my money. Meddlesome bitch," Carter said.

"Insincere and unethical jackass," she retorted.

Stanley stiffened at the insult, while Harold snorted a laugh.

The ping was loud in the ensuing silence. He looked at his phone and then smiled. "It's a lovely day." Harold reached for his gun.

Roman slipped his phone back in a pocket then tightened the strap on his vest. He had to hand it to Israel: the man kept a small arsenal in his trunk, including bulletproof vests. Quiet footsteps scuffed behind him.

"TJ has sent the funds, and it will hold up under the initial scrutiny. Once he tries to move the money, he'll have nothing but goose eggs," Roman reported.

Israel squatted next to Roman, out of sight of the building. "He has her bound in a backroom. She's pretty banged up but holding steady." He checked his weapon. "Let's get his attention then bring our woman home."

Tires crunched on gravel. Roman grabbed Israel and dragged the man to the ground. The two flattened behind the van as a Mercedes skidded to a halt, a cloud of dust settling in its wake. A man shoved out of the vehicle and jogged to the building.

"Shit. Who was that?" Israel asked.

"That was one of the partners," Roman answered. "The Stanley guy Cailyn mentioned."

"He's behind this?"

"I think so."

"We're gonna need a distraction." Crouching, Israel patted his pockets, coming up with a switchblade and a lighter.

"I was gonna bust the windows out of the van," Roman suggested.

"Sure thing."

Using an ASP—a telescoping baton—Roman smashed the van window. The alarm blared to life. Israel used a switchblade on a rear tire before scrambling to the Mercedes.

"The fool left his doors unlocked."

Roman kept watch. "Whatcha got in mind?"

Israel popped the button for the fuel tank, unscrewed the cap, and shoved a rag into the opening.

"You're nuts."

Israel grinned like a loon. "And it's at a quarter tank." He waited until the rag was wet then lit the wick. They ran for cover.

Inside, Harold whirled at the sound of glass and then the horn blaring. "What the..." He glared at Stanley. "Who else is in on this?"

"You and me."

Harold lunged at the man. "Liar!" The two men locked together as an explosion rocked the building. Glass shards blew inward. Cailyn managed a scream as she rolled behind some old crates.

"My car!" Stanley screamed. Footsteps pounded on the floor, followed by the sound of a lone gunshot.

She lay there on the floor, blinking. The unmistakable sound of crackling fire, along with burning rubber, filled the air. She sniffed as thick gray smoke floated in. *What in the world?* Cautiously, she peered around the crates. No one was in the room.

Cailyn shifted. Did she have time to even get out of the room? The tape at her wrists still held fast. If she could inch her way toward the door, she might have a chance.

Slowly, painfully, she inched her way across the floor, using the wall as a guide. Running footsteps brought her up short. She swung her head in the direction of the noise. There was another door, one she had not seen.

Something heavy struck the wood and she managed to stifle a scream. A moment later the wood splintered and the door fell inward. Roman stood in the entryway.

"Roman!" She sagged with relief. "How'd you find me?"

He crossed to her, flipping a switchblade into position as he did. He knelt and made short work of the tape. "Can you walk?"

"I think so," she admitted. "My head is spinning and I really want to throw up."

He reached down and hauled her to her feet. She wobbled in his arms, but he held on until she was steady.

"He killed Paul. Carter Stanley is involved," she babbled, stepping forward. Immediately the world tilted and the floor threatened to meet her. She grabbed the wall to steady herself. "What was that explosion?"

"Israel letting off steam."

"You sent the money." She clamped a hand over her mouth. Oh god, she didn't want to be sick again. Several deep breaths dispelled the persistent nausea. Barely.

Rome tapped his earpiece. "Rael, I've got the package. She's in bad shape." Rome slid his free hand around her waist.

Cailyn clutched at his shirt, determined to stay on her feet. Her men needed her strong right now, regardless of her injuries. "I can do this, Roman."

He brushed a kiss on the top of her head. "I know. You are woman, hear you roar."

Gunshots rang out. Roman moved her behind him. "When I move, you move," he said quietly.

She pressed closer to him. "I'm so sorry I ever found those discrepancies."

He glanced at her, a half-smile on his face. "But you'll do it again."

"It's who I am."

A loud thump hit the wall and they froze. Rome indicated for Cailyn to crouch down. He then pulled a couple of empty fifty-gallon drums in front of her.

"No!" she hissed.

"Israel's not answering me," Roman told her.

Another gunshot rang out and was followed by a cry of rage.

"Where's my money?"

"Shit! The jig is up." Roman reached between the drums and hauled Cailyn to her feet. "Stay low. Stay behind me."

She followed him, doing her best to ignore the nausea and double vision. They had just one more corridor to traverse and they were home free. She could see cracks of sunlight streaking through broken, dirty window panes, an open door just beyond. The only thing separating them from freedom was one hundred feet of open floor.

Behind them and to the left, a door banged open.

"I'll kill her," Harold raged.

Cailyn stumbled. Roman caught her up and shoved her in front of him.

Sixty feet.

Israel appeared in the open doorway. "I lost him."

"He's behind us," Roman said.

Forty feet.

"She has a concussion," Roman told him.

Thirty feet.

Israel widened his eyes. Cailyn wasn't sure what happened next. Everything slowed down. Pain rocked her body at the same instant noise shrouded her senses.

She gasped for air as the oxygen left her lungs in a whoosh. Israel tucked and rolled her, coming up on one knee. His body jerked and he fell backward.

Something warm hit her face. Someone was screaming, but it was far away. She rolled to her side, every cell in her body protesting the move. She looked up, her vision swimming. She blinked, only to stare into two round barrels that slowly morphed into one smoking gun.

She couldn't move. A growl, a primitive cry of a male protecting his mate, filled the air. Rome tackled the man just as he pulled the trigger.

Cailyn dropped to the ground.

CHAPTER FOURTEEN

Here they were in another hospital room, this one iden-
tical to the first with the exception of the window facing
a wooded area. The blinds were open and a patch of blue-
black velvet sky sliced through the glass. Israel tightened
his grip on the IV pole. He had half a mind to pull out the
needle but decided against the irritant. He could shoulder
the discomfort a while longer. What he couldn't stand was
this stupid hospital gown. Instead of walking around with
his ass out, he'd commandeered a pair of scrub bottoms
to go with the gown. The brown grippy socks made little
noise on the linoleum. He stepped fully into Cailyn's room.

Israel surveyed the man sprawled between the window
seat and chair. A bandage peeked beneath the short-sleeve
t-shirt. A lump lodged in his throat. If not for this man, he
would be dead. Roman opened his eyes.

"How is she?" Israel asked.

Roman sat up, wincing as he did. He removed his feet from the chair. "Sleeping. They had to give her a mild sedative." He indicated the now empty chair and eyed him skeptically. "Shouldn't you be in bed?"

"Probably, but I've been shot before." Gratefully Israel sat. Every muscle thanked him for the respite. His wound was a through and through. Only luck had the bullet missing bone and any major veins or arteries. "You saved my life."

There had been nowhere for Israel to run or even time to duck. It hadn't even mattered that he wore a Kevlar vest. The only thing that mattered was saving Cailyn.

Roman had the presence of mind to shove Cailyn forward. Israel caught her, rolling her beneath his body as the first bullet fired. He could remember the heat singeing his ear. By the time he came up on one knee, a second bullet knocked him on his back and left him with a nice hole in his shoulder. He nodded a chin to Roman's bandage. "Shouldn't you be in bed?"

"I only required stitches. You, on the other hand, needed a surgeon and a pint of blood."

"You saved my life," Israel repeated.

"Consider the debt repaid."

Israel leaned forward to lay his hand on Cailyn's. "You saved her too."

"And have you pissed off at me for the rest of my life?" he demanded.

Israel snorted. "I can't believe he actually shot us."

"I can't believe he almost got away with it."

"You're both here," came the quiet, sleepy voice.

"Where else would we be?" Israel demanded, moving his chair closer to the bed.

"Chasing bad guys," she said.

Roman chuckled, unashamedly wiping his tears away. "You're supposed to be sleeping."

"You saved my life." She flicked her gaze between them. "Both of you."

Israel squeezed gently on her fingers. "We love you. We could do no less."

She shifted and bit back a groan of pain. "Did I get shot?"

"A bullet grazed you, but those are cracked ribs, baby girl," Israel said.

"They wouldn't let me see you guys." She licked dry lips.

Roman picked up a Styrofoam cup with a bendy straw from the rolling table and placed the straw at her lips. She drank a couple of sips of the cool liquid. Amazing how a few sips of water could revitalize her system. He raised a brow and she shook her head. He set the water aside then sat on her other side.

"Or tell me how you were doing." She let out a careful breath. "They thought I was hysterical and..."

"Yeah, the nurses say you gave them hell until they knocked you out." Roman grinned.

"I'd have loved to see that," Israel teased. "Our quiet Cailyn giving the nurses hell."

"My brain is all fuzzy," Cailyn admitted. "What happened after I passed out?"

"I tackled Harold. Once he realized he couldn't shoot you and he couldn't kill himself, he pretty much gave up." Roman smoothed back her hair. "He's in custody. Rael and I got to answer a whole bunch of questions and fill out a helluva lot of paperwork."

"Yep. That's why I like working for myself. Don't have to deal with the bureaucratic bullshit," Israel joked.

"And Carter Stanley?" Cailyn asked.

Roman grinned. "Harold shot him."

Cailyn gasped.

Israel patted her hand. "Don't worry. He's not dead. But he wishes he was."

"TJ returned the money. You will receive a reward for your diligent services, and my job is there if I want it," Roman finished.

"I've never been so terrified in my life," she admitted. "I really thought I was going to die."

Israel moved to her other side, while Roman crowded in on the other. "We weren't going to let that happen," Israel reminded her.

Tears leaked from her eyes and she didn't try to brush them away. "If I'd known Paul was involved, I'd never have had you look for him." This she said to Roman. "The guy hit us. He started shooting at anyone who tried to interfere."

"He had us all fooled. I'd have done the same thing," Roman assured her.

She shook her head. "He shot him. He shot Paul right in front of me."

The two men exchanged twin looks of pain and regret across the bed.

"You survived," Roman said gently.

"You're alive, baby," Israel soothed.

"He was so callous about killing him. The worst thing was I believed him when he said he really didn't want to hurt me, but he would." She touched each man, assuring herself they were real and alive. "And you were both hurt."

"We'll heal," Israel promised vehemently. "Just like you will. No matter how long it takes, we'll be here for you."

"Absolutely." Roman smoothed her hair from her face. "Now we need you to calm down before the nurse comes in and tries to kick us out."

Israel handed her a tissue.

"This is about as calm as I'm going to get right now." She hiccupped and dashed at the tears. "I can't seem to stop crying."

Roman stroked her fingers, the swelling not as pronounced as before. "Then keep crying. You've been through a traumatic experience."

She chuckled despite her tears. "You're always so reasonable and logical."

"You should've seen him earlier. He was nowhere near reasonable or logical," Israel told her.

"How would you know," Roman mumbled. "You were shot."

Israel grinned, enjoying the other man's discomfort. "I still had to pull you off that asshole. You were beating the crap outta him."

"You'd have beat the crap outta him too if the roles were reversed," he shot back defensively.

"Nope. I'd have emptied a clip in him, reloaded, and done it again."

The statement was delivered so nonchalantly the other two had to stare at Israel.

"What?" He feigned innocence. "I can't lose the best woman ever or my oldest friend again."

Cailyn swiped at more tears. "You're both dorks."

They burst out laughing.

She squeezed their hands. "Stay with me."

And they did.

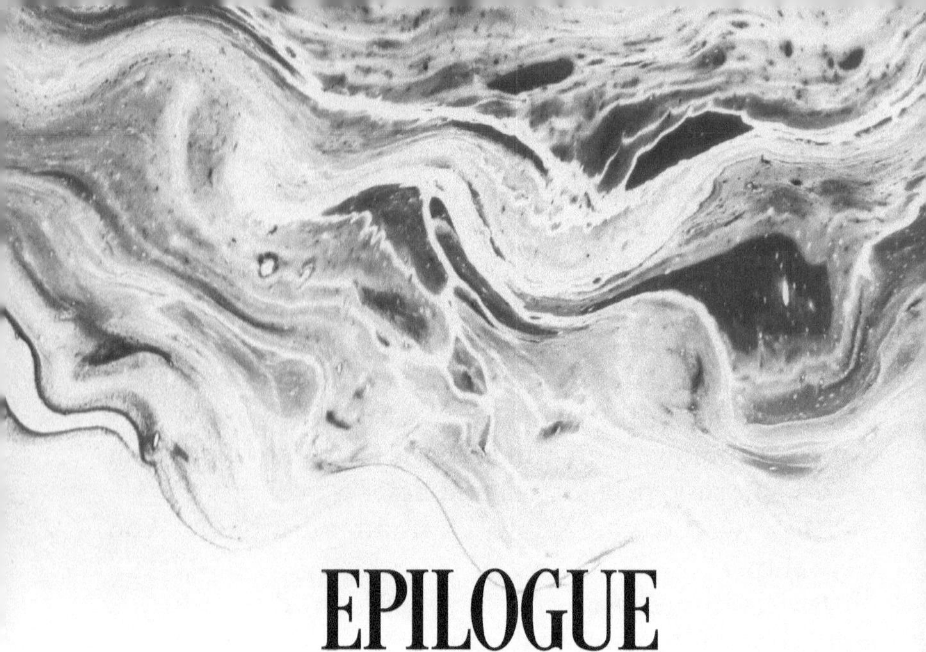

EPILOGUE

A Few Weeks Later

Two men sat on the covered lanai overlooking a quiet expanse of water. Gentle waves rippled and broke against the floating dock. The fifty feet of canal flowed into the Gulf of Mexico. In the fading sunlight, a few sailboats and jet skis could be seen in the distance. One man, the taller of the two, stood and crossed to a small grill. He lifted the lid and dense gray smoke billowed out along with the scent of roasted meat.

He prodded the thick steaks, flipped them, then closed the lid before resuming his seat.

"You've got a really sweet setup here," Roman mused. "No wonder she loves being here so much."

Once Cailyn was discharged from the hospital, she'd spent the time in Israel's home, while Roman split his time between his condo and Israel's.

"She spent a lot of time on the dock." Israel pointed to an empty chaise toward the end. "The water seems to soothe her."

Roman glanced toward the closed sliders. "Is she still having trouble sleeping?"

Israel shifted, his shoulder giving a muted protest. "Only when she's alone. She sleeps better when one or both of us are in the bed with her."

Roman nodded. Since he'd spent so much time with Cailyn, he and Israel had garnered not quite an uneasy truce, but definitely a truce.

"And how are you feeling about all this time I'm spending at your place?" He made the question as nonchalant as possible.

Israel sipped his beer to buy time. They still had issues to resolve, but nothing insurmountable. Instead of going on the defensive, he decided on the truth. "It's been nice having my friend around again." He saw the momentary flash of surprise on Roman's face and he rushed on. "But I'll do anything to keep Cailyn happy."

Roman hid a smile behind his own bottle. "Understood."

They fell silent. After a few minutes, Roman returned to the grill and flipped the steaks again. They would be ready soon.

"I love her more than any woman I have ever loved before," Israel said when Roman resumed his seat. "I would ask her to marry me if I knew she would say yes."

Roman swigged his beer. "She's not a monogamous woman," he pointed out. "You would never be the only man in her life."

They fell silent, the occasional pop and hiss of the grill the only sound.

"How are you so easy with this?" Israel wanted to know. "After everything that's happened, the arguments and disagreements. The betrayal…"

Roman sighed. "I've known who I am for a long time. Whether I'm with one woman or three, I'm happy with that. I was happier when we shared a woman we were both attracted to." He shrugged. "I even managed to be happy not sharing a woman with you, Rael. Having two women at the same time is pretty hot."

Israel smirked. "What haven't you done?"

Roman pretended to give it some thought. "Suck another man's dick."

Israel burst out laughing.

He grinned. "I definitely prefer women, but if you were the last man on Earth, I'd make you my bitch."

A sliding door opened, cool air rushing forward, and both men turned. Cailyn exited the house, holding a tray laden with bowls of salad, corn, and potatoes. She smiled.

"Well the two of you seem to be getting along."

Israel set down his bottle, rose, and hurried to help her with the tray, even though his shoulder wasn't one hundred percent. Cailyn was still nursing a sprained wrist and cracked ribs. She shouldn't have been carrying the tray at all. He sent her a disapproving frown.

When he was close enough, she kissed his cheek. Roman stood as well but went toward the grill.

"Just catching up on old times," Israel said, taking the tray from her. "And that little peck on the cheek does not absolve you."

"Then I'll have to think of something else." She walked her fingers up his biceps.

"Steaks are done," Roman announced.

Israel set the tray on the table then caught Cailyn by the hand and drew her close. "You are the most intelligent, beautiful, loving woman I've met in a long time."

"It sounds like you're buttering me up for something," she teased.

"Maybe I am," he mumbled. He glanced at Roman.

"It's your idea. You ask her," he said.

"What kinda friend are you?" Israel groused.

"The kind who lets you stand on your own two feet," Roman said.

Cailyn placed her hand on a chair. "Well, while the two of you figure out what you want to say, I'm going to have a seat."

Roman pulled the steaks off the grill, while Israel sat in the chair next to Cailyn. He dished out salad, while Roman placed a steak next to the potatoes and corn.

"I'd like you to move in with me," he blurted.

"Oh." What else could she say? She had no intentions of returning to her apartment. Even though her room had been professionally cleaned and a new bed had been purchased, there was no way she could sleep in the same room where a man had been violently murdered. Not after witnessing Paul's death. Nightmares of that, as well as her abduction, plagued her.

Spending the last few weeks recuperating at Israel's home and having Roman stay had begun to feel natural to her.

"Israel and I have been talking," Rome began.

Israel sent him a glare.

"Fine. You tell her," Rome said with a chuckle.

Cailyn studied each man in turn. Roman sat with a smug expression on his handsome face, while Israel held the same vulnerability she'd seen in him the night he'd given her the emerald necklace and earrings. She touched his hand. "What is it?"

"Rome and I have been talking," he agreed. "We don't have everything settled, but we... Well I think it would be nice if you'd move in with me," he rushed on. "Rome would keep his condo for now, but he would spend time here as well.

"There's plenty of room, and when Rome and I start to clash, one or the other can go to the condo," Israel finished. "Or you can go to the condo if we get on your nerves."

She smiled at this.

The silence stretched and Israel shook his head. "I told you she wouldn't go for it."

Cailyn placed a hand on Roman's arm before he could respond. "Why wouldn't I?"

Israel stared at her, a flicker of hope in his hazel eyes. "Because I'm still a bit insecure and a hothead."

"Admitting you have a problem is the first step of recovery," Roman quipped.

Israel flipped him off.

Cailyn chuckled. "If you're serious."

He opened his mouth to agree and she placed a finger across his lips.

"If you're serious and we can all agree on a schedule, I will move in with you."

He grinned. Again Cailyn placed a silencing finger over his lips.

"I will be committed to you and Roman as my primary partners. Right now that's enough for me."

"And when it's not enough?" Roman asked.

She held Israel's gaze as she answered the question. "Then we'll discuss it."

Israel kissed her fingertip. "I can live with that."

"Me too. Let's eat."

To Be Continued...

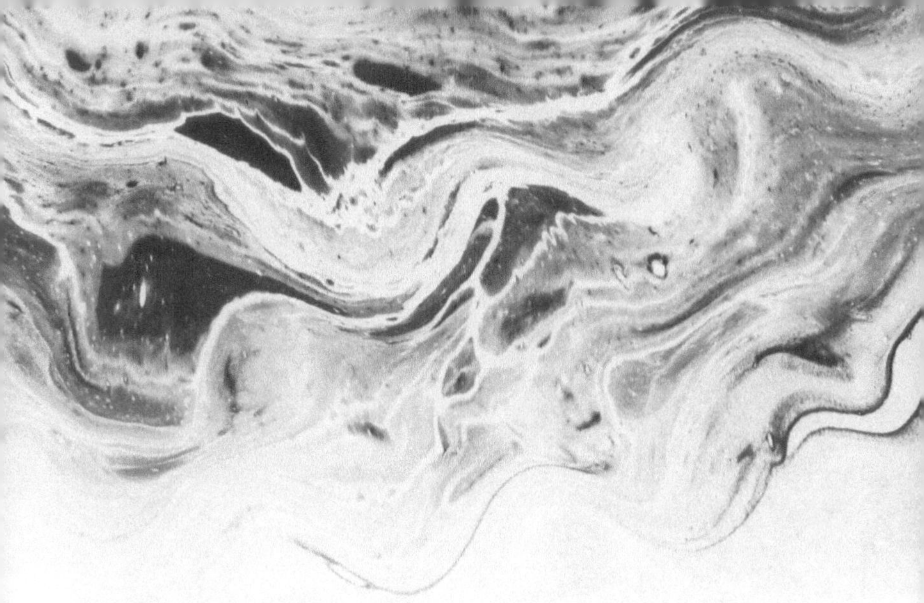

BOOK CLUB QUESTIONS

1. Why do you think the book is titled *The Kink Brothers*?

2. Do you think Cailyn handled Israel's insecurity well? What could she have done differently?

3. Do you know where the names Flopsie and Mopsie came from?

4. What did you think of TJ?

5. How would you handle a poly or non-monogamous relationship?

AUTHOR BIO

Lynn Chantale, the brilliant architect of heart-throbbing romance, master of electrifying short stories, and enchantress whose soulful voice occasionally graces the background of musical masterpieces, has set the literary world ablaze with her passionate tales. Her oeuvre is a treasure trove of unforgettable experiences, featuring pulse-pounding narratives like "Sex, Lies, and Joysticks," the captivating "True Detective Series," and the soul-stirring "Broken Lens," just to name a few.

When she's not crafting tales that set the pages on fire, Lynn is ruling her own kingdom with an iron fist, reigning supreme over her bustling household, her beloved family, and her feline companion, none other than the illustrious Shakespeare. You can catch up with Lynn and bask in the enchantment of her words at any of her online sanctuaries, where the magic of her storytelling knows no bounds.

**Discover more at
4HorsemenPublications.com**

10% off using HORSEMEN10

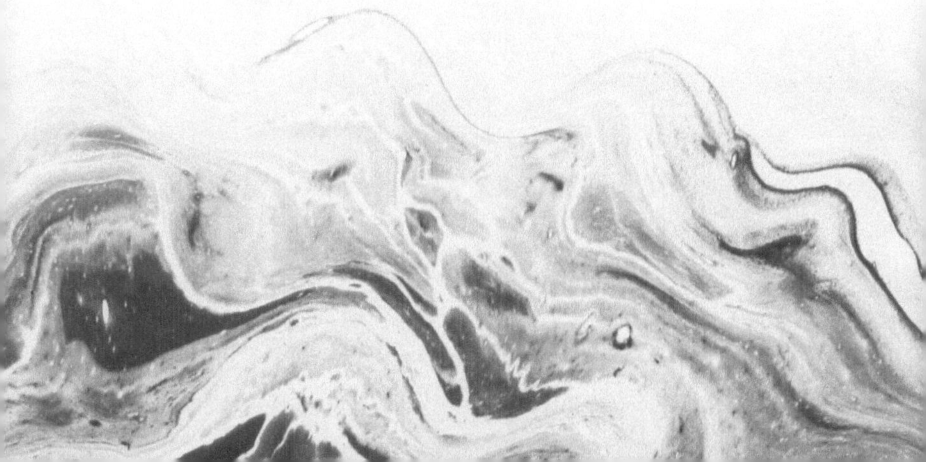